THE VENGEANCE OF BOON HELM

Texan Boon Helm rides bravely into Mexico's heart of darkness, which is ruled by ruthless killers. And, joined at the border hotel by a voluptuous lady in search of love, he hopes that her gun-toting husband won't turn up! Boon, seeking to avenge his best friend's murder, risks being beaten, tortured and imprisoned. As explosions crash out and the body count spirals, can he fight through and take one of his many women along for the ride?

Books by Henry Remington in the Linford Western Library:

A MAN CALLED SLAUGHTER
DEATH IN DURANGO
MORGAN'S WAR
SHOOT-OUT AT SAN LORENZO

HENRY REMINGTON

THE VENGEANCE OF BOON HELM

Complete and Unabridged

LINFORD
Leicester

First published in Great Britain in 2010 by
Robert Hale Limited
London

First Linford Edition
published 2012
by arrangement with
Robert Hale Limited
London

British Library CIP Data

Remington, Henry.
The vengeance of Boon Helm. - -
(Linford western library)
1. Americans- -Mexico- -Fiction. 2. Revenge
- -Fiction. 3. Murder- -Fiction. 4. Western
stories. 5. Large type books.
I. Title II. Series
823.9′2–dc23

ISBN 978–1–4448–1095–0

Published by
F. A. Thorpe (Publishing)
Anstey, Leicestershire

Set by Words & Graphics Ltd.
Anstey, Leicestershire
Printed and bound in Great Britain by
T. J. International Ltd., Padstow, Cornwall

This book is printed on acid-free paper

1

'C'm on, moke. Just one more load to take into town an' you an' me are gonna retire an' put our feet up for a bit.' The gnarled old-timer, Jed Joplin, groaned as he hefted a pannier of ore onto the back of the *burro*, hooking it to the wooden *apparejo*. 'It'll be a rockin' chair and a bottle of hooch for me and all the hay you wanna eat.'

Joplin was working in the tunnel of the Shirt Tail mine, shovelling up any silver-streaked chunks of ore they might have missed. For years he had been wandering from one stampede to the next across the West, from California to Pike's Peak, until he had struck paydirt at Tombstone. For six months, ore from the Shirt Tail had paid out at $250 to the ton.

But the ancient desert rat and his young partner, Boon Helm, had agreed only yesterday to accept an offer from a mystery bidder to sell out. Tomorrow the mine would be handed over. Jed scratched at his white beard, tugged his battered hat down over his brow and caught hold of the *burro*'s head collar, trundling with him towards the entrance of the mine.

Suddenly, a man stepped into the tunnel silhouetted against the fierce sunlight. His high-heeled boots and sombrero made him stand tall. There was a threat to his manner that made the sweat soaking the shirt on Jed's back turn icy cold.

'Yeah?' he croaked out. 'Whadda ya want?'

He could not make out the *hombre*'s features but the sun's rays struck on the silver rings pinning the sides of his wide leather *chaparejos*. And off the silver-engraved six-gun in his hand.

'Why you not make a guess, *señor*?' The Mexican gave a cold-hearted laugh.

The miner stared into the deathly

hole of the barrel of the gun then gasped out, 'Clear off. Go to hell. There ain't nuthin' for you here.' He snatched a chunk of ore from the pannier, hurled it at the intruder, grabbed a shovel and swung, viciously, at his wrist in an attempt to disarm him.

'*Hijo de puta*!' The *hombre* cried out with pain as the shovel sliced into his wrist, but back-stepping to avoid another enraged swing by the desperate Joplin, fired point blank. The *burro* started away as the explosion racketed through the tunnel and the miner toppled onto his back.

'You devil's spawn,' Jed coughed out, as he lay there, blood oozing from his shirt. 'Curse you!'

For reply the killer stepped closer, pressed the revolver barrel into the beard beneath Jed's chin and hissed, 'So long, *amigo*.' His second bullet tore the old man's head apart in a mess of blood and bone.

The Mexican met the *burro*'s puzzled eyes as black powdersmoke drifted and shrugged. 'He asked for it. Now, where he keep his stuff? Ha! A pity you do not talk.'

But he did not have to search for long as he went further into the tunnel and found a lantern and blankets where the miners had bedded down. Half-concealed in a niche in the rock wall was a tin trunk. The man's eyes gleamed with greed as he creaked the lid open. He took a pouch heavy with coins and a thick wallet from inside. He flicked a thumb through the wad of US treasury banknotes. 'Ah! Just like he said.'

He turned on his heel and strode out of the mine, leaping on his mustang and heading back into Tombstone.

* * *

Tombstone had been founded and named by another old desert rat, Ed Schieffelin, who for years had been poking round the remote areas of southern Arizona in defiance of the ravages of warring Apaches. Army patrols had ordered him out of the area, but he had ignored them. His tenacity rewarded him for in 1878 he struck 'the holy grail'. Rich seams of silver ran beneath these denuded hills.

Ed had summoned his old partner, Jed Joplin, and together they had carved out the first mines. 'Them soldier boys told me all I would find was my own tombstone,' Schieffelin cackled. 'Even them 'Pache savages seemed to think I was crazy and left me alone. So, I'm gonna name this spot Tombstone. Ironic, doncha think?'

It certainly was. Looked like the Big Dealer in the sky was paying out for Ed. He couldn't stop hauling out top-grade ore from his mine. And Jed, too, was doing OK as he dynamited into an adjacent hillside. Ed had chosen the prime location in the area where a rich seam of silver came close to the surface. It was bonanza time.

Soon as the news leaked out the rush was on. Grizzled old prospectors and city guys who'd never swung a pick in their lives arrived from far and wide, hopeful to make their fortunes. In their wake came honest merchants who sensed the chance of making money from the miners. And less-honest whiskey-sellers, tavern keepers, pimps with wagonloads of prostitutes, gamblers and outlaws coming up through the bloodsoaked canyons from Mexico.

Soon the tents of the prospectors had given way to a small town of ramshackle stores and clapboard houses on each side of a wide sunbaked main street. Today being the Sabbath the miners had downed tools and headed into town to spend their hard-gotten gains at the saloons, brothels and gaming hells where, as they say, the barleycorn flows . . .

* * *

Somebody had tipped off the *Tombstone Clarion* so the sale of the Shirt Tail for $5,000 was front-page news.

The money had been paid out, it was reported, by an attorney on behalf of a secret purchaser to the mine's co-owners.

So, when the lanky young Texan, Boon Helm, strolled into the Alhambra at noon he was greeted by an inquisitive crowd. 'What you gonna do with all that cash?' the saloon-keeper, Hal Carpenter, queried.

'For starters I'm gonna stand a round of drinks for everybody in the house,' Boon drawled. This was greeted with cheers as the crush of men called out their orders.

It had seemed eminent sense to sell out. The rich seams they had so far hacked into with reasonable profit had headed deep under the hillside. There was little more they could do without bringing in heavy equipment for hard rock deep shaft mining.

'A lot of the big syndicates are moving in,' Hal reflected. 'I think you did the right thing. So what are you really planning to do, Boon?'

'There's some fine land up in the

wilds of Colorado just waiting to be claimed. Maybe I'll start my own spread. That would be a dream of mine come true.'

'Good. I'm glad you ain't gonna waste it all on whiskey and wild wimmin. Presumably you've put your share in the bank for safe keeping?'

'No, cain't say I have. Jed don't believe in banks. Since they all went bust in '74 with folks panicking to get their cash, a lot of people feel the same way. Most don't even trust paper money but the greenbacks they paid out to us seem solid enough.'

'So, what have you done with your two an' a half thousand? Surely you ain't got it stuffed in your back pocket?'

'No, Hal. Jed's got it stashed away safe enough in his tin box. Along with what we've earned this past six months. We're gonna have a share-out tomorrow.'

The young Texan had grinned, sweeping off his well-worn Stetson, spinning it expertly to land on a coat hook where he had hung his gunbelt. He brushed back the thick fawn hair from across his brow with his hand. 'I've just brought out a hundred dollars which I'm going to invest in a poker game. Might as well have some fun. Maybe it's my lucky day.'

'So where,' the saloon-keeper asked, 'has Jed gotten to?'

'Aw, you know what he's like, a very careful man. He's back at the mine scraping up what bits of ore he can salvage before the handover.'

Two hours later he was sitting amid a bunch of poker players studying his hand as they whiled away the hot afternoon. Suddenly a Mexican youth, José Ramos, burst into the saloon. 'Señor Joplin. He dead. I find him in pool of blood.'

'You mean Jed?'

Boon stood, as if in a trance, reaching for his cartridge gunbelt from the hook to buckle loosely around his faded denim jeans. The single-action Frontier with its staghorn grip hung snugly below his slim right hip. He grabbed his hat and buckskin jacket. 'I'll go take a look.'

He raced his sturdy piebald out of town at a gallop along a winding trail, José, on a moth-eaten mule, eating his dust. By the time the latter arrived at the Shirt Tail mine Boon was already down on one knee bent over the body.

'Poor ol' Jed.' He studied what was left of his grey-bearded head. 'He didn't deserve this. He was a good old guy.'

He pressed a thumb and forefinger to his own eyes to try to stop the tears from coming. 'He was more like a father to me,' he said, blinking them away.

'Look, *señor*,' José said, a bullet in the palm of his hand. 'It must have gone through his head and ricocheted.'

Boon got to his feet and sniffed at it. 'This was fired about two hours ago' — he looked down at the corpse — 'and I'm gonna find whoever did this. I swear to that. Then it will be him or me.'

He noticed a glint of metal to one side and picked up a silver buckle. 'He must have lost this.'

'*Sí*, like *vaquero* wear to clip together leather sides of *chaparejos*.'

'Yep,' Boon mused. 'I find a man with a missing silver buckle, I find the killer.'

He picked up a shovel. 'There's a fresh bloodstain on the edge. There must have been a tussle. I figure Jed was standing here with his moke when whoever it was arrived. He took a swipe to try to disarm him, caught him, probably on the forearm, but paid the price.'

'*Madre de Dios*!' José crossed himself. 'Fancy dying when he had just struck it rich.'

'Yeah. How come you found him, José?'

'I am passing. I see his *burro* wandering free but still with pannier of ore on his side. I theenk, thees ess ver' strange. I go in. Agh! Here he is.'

'You see anybody around? Anybody

on the trail as you came along?'

'A couple miners. A woman with goat. Nothing suspicious.'

'You didn't hear the gunshots?'

'*Señor*, there are many explosions of gunpowder in the mines.'

'Right. Let's go see.'

Boon strode along the tunnel to where they would bed down and his heart began hammering as he saw the tin box on the floor, its lid open, empty. He picked it up and tossed it away. 'Looks like I ain't a wealthy man no more. There was near on five thou' in that box, plus gold and silver we had saved.'

'Whoo!' José gave another whistle of awe. 'How did the killer know where —?'

A stab of pain creased through Boon. 'Maybe he overheard me. I shot my mouth off. This morning. I shouldn't have. Perhaps I am the one to blame for this.'

'*Señor*, you should not — '

'Maybe not,' Boon muttered, but he knew that for a long time to come he would feel guilty about the old man's death. 'Come on, give me a hand to lift him. I gotta take him back and bury him.'

* * *

News of the bloody murder of the old desert rat had spread. Many had known Joplin personally. An angry crowd of about fifty men was waiting for Boon Helm when he rode in with the body slung over the *burro*.

'Who dunnit?' a miner shouted, a noose dangling from his hand. 'We want him.' The rope remedy was much in favour.

Boon raised a hand to quieten them. 'All I know for now is somebody shot the holy hell outa poor old Jed and stole all our cash. I'm gonna find out who. There's no need to get up a necktie party. Anyhow, I guess whoever it was is far away from here by now. I'm gonna give Jed Joplin a Christian burial then I'm going after his killer, I don't care how far he goes. One day I'll catch up with him. Anybody got a Bible I can borrow?'

They sewed up Joplin's body in a tarpaulin shroud and carried him on their shoulders along to Boot Hill, the graveyard where many wooden crosses looked out over the blustery plain. Most of the residents seemed to have had violent deaths with words burned into the boards simply saying, 'Hanged' — 'Stabbed' — 'Shot' — 'Drowned' — 'Buried in shaft fall'.

Another read, 'Hanged by mistake. He was right. We was wrong. But we strung him up. And now he's gone.'

'Jed was a good man, respected by all who knew him,' Boon intoned. 'Honest, hard-working, sober and true. He's been cheated out of the due rewards of his labour. May he find rest at last in the Other World. Ashes to ashes and dust to dust — '

'If the wimmin don't git ya,' a miner chimed in, 'the licker must.'

They all laughed, or shook their

heads, tamped down the grave and headed back to the saloons.

'What shall I do with the *burro, señor*?'

'You keep him, if you want, José. I don't reckon Jed had any kin we'll ever know of.' Boon jumped onto the sidewalk to push through the batwing doors of the Alhambra. 'Thanks for your help.'

'*Adios, amigo*,' José called. 'Good luck.'

* * *

Boon headed away up the street towards the jail-house and office of the town's first sheriff, a man called Slaughter. He was an odd individual, part Comanche with black hair hanging over a monolithic face, sprawled in a swivel chair, boots up on his desk.

'Guess I gotta report the facts to you.'

'You got him neatly dead an' buried now. What the hell am I s'posed to do?'

'You were outa town before, collecting taxes they said.'

'That's part of the lousy job.' Slaughter took a bottle from the desk drawer and refilled his glass. 'Strikes me I oughta arrest you. You come in here with some cock 'n bull story about a Mexican. How do I know you didn't kill your partner earlier this morning at the mine afore you come into town?'

Boon knew this man had a history of killings himself, as a former bounty hunter, and was not a person to be crossed. But he fired up, hotly. 'You take that back, you lousy — '

'So you could keep all the cash.' Slaughter fingered the Schofield across his loins. 'You ever drawn on a man before?'

Boon met the sheriff's hard green eyes. 'No.'

'No, you don't seem the sort, but human nature's a funny thing. So, what you expect me to do? Get up a posse? Go after this so-called *vaquero*? On what evidence? A silver *chaparejo* ring?'

'OK, I'll handle this alone.'

'You're crazy, kid. I oughta lock you up for your own safety. You go south of the border, those people, they'll eat you alive.'

'So, I'm free to go?'

'Sure.' Slaughter grinned. 'Get outa here. If there were any bounty on him it might be a different matter.'

* * *

The young Texan decided to make a few more enquiries before setting out and returned to the Alhambra.

The saloon-keeper saw Boon coming and poured a tumbler of whiskey for him. 'It's on the house.'

'Thanks, Hal.' He took a good slug and the liquid burned through him. 'It's been a bit of a shock.'

'Yeah, I guess it has.'

'Tell me, did you notice any nefarious-looking characters in here earlier on?'

'Sure,' Hal laughed. 'Most of my customers.'

'No, you know, a shootist? A hardcase.'

'There was a Mex I ain't seen before. A tall, mean-looking character. Didn't say much, just took a good bite outa a bottle of tequila. He was hanging around when you first came in. Didn't you notice him?'

'No, can't say I did. Everybody was crowding round me.'

'He was standing behind you just kinda listening to what was going on. Must have gone some other place after that. Next time I noticed him I was standing outside getting some air just after the kid, José, came in and you two rode out to the mine. The Mex came outa the Golden Garter opposite. He must have seen you go.'

'What did he do?'

'Jumped on his mustang and rode off in the other direction as if all the devils in Hell were after him.'

'Maybe I should mention that to the sheriff. Aw, what's the use? Ach!' The strong whiskey curdled in Boon's empty stomach. 'What did he look like?'

‘Well, you know, in range leathers, *vaquero*-style. Looked like he could handle himself. Cut your throat for a quarter. Oh, yeah, he had a scar down one cheek.’ Hal scratched a fingernail down the right side of his face. ‘A knife souvenir, and one of them pointy black sombreros like a witch’s hat.’

‘Silver buckles on his chaps?’

‘Yes, I believe that’s right. He your man?’

‘I dunno.’ Boon shrugged. ‘I’d rather you kept this to yourself the mood the miners are in.’

‘Of course, pal. Don’t want any innocent Latinos strung up, do we?’

‘Which way did he go?’

‘Towards Bisbee. You’ve left it a bit late. He’s got a three hour start on you.’

‘Why didn’t you let me know this soon as I got in with Jed’s body?’

‘I got a business to run.’ Hal Carpenter made a grimace of his lips. ‘You asked; I’ve told you. You going after him?’

‘Yes. I gotta act fast.’

Boon downed the coffin varnish and hurried outside to his horse hitched to the rail outside the Alhambra. 'C'm on, boy,' he said, swinging onto the saddle, 'there ain't gonna be no nice warm stable for us tonight.'

Straight-backed, he rode out of Tombstone at a fast clip as the sun began its fall . . .

2

Not many travellers ventured out alone through this border country, for Geronimo and his band of Apaches were still on the prowl, leading the army a merry dance and leaving a trail of death and destruction. So the only traffic Boon encountered was the six-horse stage from Bisbee charging towards, and past him and a double wagon hauled by twenty mules at a slower pace.

The stars were shining bright in a clear night sky as he hailed the mule-skinner. 'Seen any sign of a lone Mexican riding this way?'

The skinner bummed some baccy off him before he replied. 'Yeah, some evil-looking greaser did come clipping past just after I left Bisbee. That sho' is some slope to drive this rig up I can tell ya.'

'How long ago?'

'Aw.' The 'skinner tamped his pipe

and blew out fumes. 'About two or three hours ago. We got a heavy load on here.' He uncoiled his twenty-foot bullwhip and snaked it cracking over the mules' ears to go lumbering on his way. 'So long.'

Boon saw what he meant when he got his first glimpse of the lights of Bisbee. The desert trail dropped down into a deep ravine and doubled back on itself, winding up to reach the town. It was late evening but there wasn't a lot of life as Boon rode in, just the murmur of voices and clatter of china and cutlery from an imposing hotel, The Copper Queen. Unusually for the area, it was built of red bricks, probably hauled in by that same wagon from distant parts. It proclaimed the riches to be obtained from copper.

It looked a mite too grand for his quarry to be dallying, but Boon decided to take a look. He hitched the piebald outside and loosened the Frontier in its holster as he climbed the steps to the foyer.

There were big oil paintings on the walls, carpeted wooden floors. Late diners, probably businessmen and executives at the mine, took their time in the restaurant as a Latino lady rippled melodies from her harp.

'Yes, sir?' a sharp-faced woman in a white blouse and long black skirt asked him. 'Can I help you?'

'Yes, I'm looking for a Mexican. He looks like this.' Boon unfolded a piece of notepaper on which he had scrawled his impression of the killer. 'A *vaquero*, with a scar.'

'Erm?' She gave a disdainful sniff. 'I doubt if such a person would be one of our clientele.'

'I'm kinda hungry,' Boon drawled, for he hadn't eaten all day. 'Any chance of some grub?'

The receptionist looked him up and down with distaste. Boon's denim shirt, his sunbleached jeans and boots were caked with desert dust and his unruly hair was badly in need of a cut.

'Possibly,' she replied. 'I'll see what the chef has to say.'

The venison steak topped with some

sort of cheese enchilada, followed by apple pie and cream, sure hit the spot. He was surprised by the lack of change from his five-dollar note. But, what the hell. He still had eighty dollars in his shirt pocket. 'Why not have a ball?' he muttered, as he rolled a cigarette and relaxed over coffee.

'Was that to your satisfaction, sir?' the lady asked as she cleared away.

'Sure, I was hungry as a hunter.'

'Not a man-hunter?' she asked.

'I guess you could say so.'

'Are you a deputy of the law by any chance?'

'No. This is a personal affair.'

Boon watched the sway of her hips as she moved away with the tray. He guessed she was pretty old, thirty-five at least, but she certainly had an attractively rounded, hour-glass figure.

'I gotta take a look around town for that bastard,' he said to himself, but stifled a yawn. It had been a long day. 'Maybe I can book a bed here for the night?' he suggested when she returned for the silver coffee pot.

Again she gave him the doubting once-over. 'You might find more suitable accommodation in one of the *cantinas* or saloons along the ravine.'

'Nope. This'll do. How much for a room?'

'Ten dollars a night. One of our best.'

'Wow!' Boon grinned at her, widely. 'Does that include you?'

The receptionist, or hotel-keeper, or whatever she was, gave him her prim look. He caught her arm as she turned away. 'Sorry, ma'am. Just my joke.' He peeled a ten from his wad and tossed it onto her tray. 'I'll take it.'

'You can stable your horse around the back,' she said after she had provided him with a key. 'Our ostler will take care of it at no extra charge.'

'That's nice to know. I'm gonna take a nose around town.'

'We lock up at two.'

'I should be back by then,' he replied, his eyes taking on a more serious look. 'With any luck. If not, don't worry about it.'

'Don't do anything foolish,' she said. 'We don't want any trouble.'

The hotel and spacious larger villas of the wealthy soon gave way to a more sleazy side of town which was tucked along inside a rocky canyon. There were stores of various sorts, mostly closed for the night, and boxy 'dobes down twisting streets until Boon reached the slag heaps, stamps and smelting works' chimneys of the copper mines. Around a corner was Brewery Gulch, a street of saloons, cheap boarding-houses and bordellos.

The young Texan stood and steeled himself. It was true, he had never killed a man before. But he had embarked upon a matter of honour, of vengeance, and now the realization came to him that he might well have to do so, if he could. His opponent, it seemed sure, was a practised killer. If he was in any one of these rowdy saloons it might well be he, Boon, who was gunned down. He bit his lip and pushed open the door of the Miner's Rest. He guessed this was how his father felt when the infantry moved into battle in the Big War. And *he* had never come back.

The noise, the stench of cheap perfume, beef stew, sweat, tobacco, beer and whiskey, was enough to blast a man back out of the door. Boon peered through a fug of cigar smoke at a bedlam of scruffy miners, singing, laughing, shouting, shovelling booze down their throats like there was no tomorrow. The Texan stepped over a prostrate drunk and shoved his way towards the bar. 'Gimme a beer,' he shouted at full lung power.

One came sliding along the counter towards him and a slatternly girl screeched, 'That's fifty cents.'

He showed her his creased drawing. 'You seen any sign of this guy? A tall *vaquero*?'

She beckoned him to follow her into a quieter corridor. 'He was in here earlier. Hours ago. He's gawn.' There was a sheen of perspiration on her face, her thin dress stuck to her, her blonde hair bedraggled. She reached out a clawlike hand to his face. 'What you want him fer? Won't I do?'

'How much are you, another fifty cents?' He thrust a dollar into her hand. 'Keep the change.'

'Gee, thanks, kid,' she called, as he left by the back door. 'Don't go.'

'I ain't lookin' fer a dose of cupid's measles,' he muttered. 'Who's she think she is callin' me kid?'

It was the same in four other bawdy houses, if a tad less noisy. His quarry had been and gone. 'Guess he's back over the line by now,' Boon mused. There were a few Mexicans around but they didn't have the look of his man.

As he sat, morosely, sipping another beer, memories of his mother and two sisters returned to him. After his father died they had run a small laundry in his home town. Theirs had seemed the epitome of Victorian virtue and modesty. A world apart from that girl in the corridor. What would they think if they could see him now?

In the early hours he made his way back to the Copper Queen.

There was nobody around so he took his key from the hook and found his room on the first floor. It was spacious and elegant. A double candelabra was burning. There was a hip bath in the corner behind a Chinese screen and a jug of warm water. Why not? Wash away the sweat and grime of work and travel. There was a big towel to dry himself. He heard the sound of the front door down below being locked. He looked out of the window onto the plaza. A man and woman were leaving. Probably the cook and housekeeper. He pulled back the bed cover. The sheets were clean and scented. Boon rolled into them naked. This was luxury, indeed.

He was just about to lean across to extinguish the candles when there was a discreet tap on the door. His gunbelt was hung from the bedknob and he jerked the Colt Frontier .45 calibre from it. 'Yeah?'

The door opened and the receptionist lady stepped in. 'Is there anything else you need, sir?' She gave him a mocking smile. 'Why, that's quite an impressive weapon you have there. How long would that barrel be?'

'Just the regular six inches, ma'am. I clean and polish it every day.'

'Oh, that's nice,' she cooed, and locked the door from inside with a flourish. 'I do like a nice clean weapon. You didn't answer my question.'

'That depends what you're offering.' Boon's Adam's apple gulped as she undid her skirt, stepped out of it in white pantalettes and black stockings, and unbuttoned her blouse without hurry. Her bosom strained for release from an embroidered white top. 'Yeah, waal, how much is this gonna cost me?'

She removed the pantalettes and slid into the bed beside him. 'It's all part of the service,' she murmured.

Her air of icy disdain was melting as her fingers stroked his long, muscled body. There was a sparkle of humour in her blue eyes as she pouted her lips to kiss his. Her body was warm, well-formed and milky white and Boon felt like he was sinking into some sort of paradise.

'Wow,' he said, as he surfaced from the deep kiss. But he was puzzled, and asked, 'Do you own this joint?'

'No. My husband does.'

'Uh?' It jolted him awake. 'Really?'

'Don't worry. He's away on business in Tombstone. I waved goodbye as he caught the stage this afternoon.'

'That must be the stage that passed me.'

'I have no doubt.'

'Waal, ma'am, I hope he don't come home early.'

'Relax.' Her fingers slid down between his legs and she smiled as she caressed him. 'He's miles away.'

'Jeez!' Boon was almost lost for words as her fingers worked their magic. 'Do me a favour,' he groaned. 'Don't call me kid. I'm twenty-two.'

'You sure seem old enough and big enough to me, cowboy,' she replied, huskily. 'C'm on, 'bout time you were in the saddle.'

3

The only thing to show that he was crossing the frontier was a big old stone carved with the word, Mexico. On the reverse side was USA. It had probably been there since 1848 when vast swathes of the former Spanish empire, California, Arizona, New Mexico, and Texas were abandoned by General Santa Anna.

Boon urged the sprightly, high-stepping piebald on, following a dirt trail for miles through red cliff gorges and across an arid plateau of pincushion cactus and spiky yukka amid the boulders.

'I strongly advise you to go back,' the woman had urged, as they took a break from their exertions in the night and he spoke of his mission. 'The man you seek is the messenger of one of President Diaz's cronies, the local warlord who protects that area. If you interfere such men will have no hesitation in killing you.'

'Who is this warlord?'

'Don Luiz Vallejo, one of the old aristocrats, a turncoat who saved his skin by fighting for the *Juaristas* against the French. As soon as Juarez was dead in his bed he conspired with Diaz to take over the country and re-establish the old order. As a reward the new *presidente* gave him a half-a-million acre *hacienda* outside Fronteras.'

'Well, he ain't got no right coming into the States and killing my pard. All I want is my cash back.'

'Huh!' His bedmate had snorted with laughter. 'You ain't got a hope. What you gonna do? Ride in there and ask for it? You think Raoul Ramirez is gonna bother talking to some wet-behind-the-ears Texan cowboy?'

'Who's Ramirez? The messenger? The killer?'

'Mm.' She had nodded, sipping from a chilled glass of white wine from a bottle she had brought to the room. 'Yes, Don Luiz's *mayor domo*, what you would call his ramrodder, his head *vaquero*. But I doubt if Don Luiz would have ordered this execution. It's more likely Raoul acted on the spur of the moment on his own account.'

'How do you know all this?'

'I keep my ears open.'

'You sound to be pretty familiar with this Raoul.'

'He has been here to arrange business between Don Luiz and my husband.'

'What sort of business?'

'How do I know? That is my husband's business.' She had laughed again, put the glass aside, and snuggled back into him, running her fingers across his lean, muscled body and murmuring, 'My business is with you. Come along, cowboy, it is almost dawn. I will have to be up and about my duties soon. Ah, the sun is rising and so are you!'

* * *

At noon the piebald had clip-clopped him into the small town of Agua Prieta. There was a dusty square surrounded by 'dobes squatted around a towering mission church, one of the many magnificent churches raised by the Spaniards on the backs of their Indian slaves. He watered his horse at a central fountain and sat in a shady *cantina* quenching his own thirst with a glass of rusty-tasting beer.

He thought about the woman's words. Was this mission so suicidal? The odds did not look good. But he was determined to go on until his luck, or his cash, ran out. If he tightened his belt the seventy dollars he had left could last him a good while in this country where the average wage was fifty cents a week. The uncomfortable statistic also returned to him that life expectancy was exceedingly low, too, about twenty-seven years or so.

There had been a few other guests in the hotel restaurant that morning. The *madame* had been haughtily prim and proper again as she served him breakfast, just a flicker of mischief in her blue eyes. But when he left there was a sadness about her. 'Sir!' she called from the reception desk. 'Your change.' She had slid ten silver dollars back to him, and whispered, 'You may need it more than me.' She had followed him to the door and touched his arm. 'So, you are going on?' When he nodded she shrugged. 'You are a fool. Don't say I didn't warn you.'

It occurred to Boon that he didn't even know her name as he collected his horse and headed determinedly on his way. The night with the woman had made him feel good. Since the age of fourteen he had wandered through Texas, New Mexico and Arizona finding jobs where he could, wrangler, cowhand, washing dishes, digging ditches, and a spell as a stage-coach shotgun. It hadn't been easy. The South had been in ruins after the war, and the collapse of the banks hadn't helped. But he had managed to stay on the right side of the law. No, he wasn't a kid any more. He'd got a Bowie on his belt, the Frontier snug in its holster pig-stringed to his thigh, and his Spencer .53 carbine tucked in the saddle boot.

'I ain't sceered of 'em,' he muttered, although he decided it would be safer to hide sixty of his dollars in his sock. By the time he rode into Fronteras it was late evening.

* * *

Old Spanish colonial buildings hung over narrow cobbled streets where stores were still lantern lit and doing good trade. By day Fronteras was a busy market centre. Big stone arcades surrounded the main square where muleteers had hobbled their animals and appeared to be preparing to sleep out under the stars.

Boon paid a dollar to a man called Manuel for a *morral* of split corn for the piebald and was told he could bed down, himself, in the ramshackle stable.

'*Muchas gracias, señor,*' the Texan said, in the frontier Spanish he had been speaking since a boy, and asked where was a good place to eat.

The chicken leg, with its scaly claw still attached sticking up from a pile of re-fried beans flavoured with red-hot chilli pepper brought him out in a sweat, but filled his belly. He washed it down with a bottle of murky red wine. A Mexican was strumming a plangent lament from a mandolin, made from an armadillo shell, over in a corner and by midnight Boon was feeling, all in all, kinda sleepy. 'Guess I'll be hitting the hay,' he muttered.

He had shown the fat, oily-faced restaurant owner his drawing, and a couple of other customers, too, mentioning the name Rodriguez, but all he got were blank regards, shrugs or shakes of the head.

He was just getting to his feet when two *vaqueros* pushed into the saloon with a clatter of spurs. Dust covered, they looked like they had been riding hard. They wore greasy leather range clothes and flamboyant sombreros and were slung with shooting irons.

One pointed a finger at Boon and called out, 'You are the *Americano* who is asking questions?'

It was more a challenge than a question, but the *vaquero*, if somewhat arrogant, seemed polite enough. 'We understand you wish to speak to a friend of ours.'

'Maybe. Where do I find him?'

'*Señor*, this is a private matter. It would be best if we spoke in the other room.' He doffed his sombrero, smiled, and indicated an alcove. 'If you please, *señor*.'

'Sure. But just who are you?'

'My name is Louis Philippe. This is my friend, Gonzalez.' The *hombre* smiled like an alligator. 'We can help you.'

'OK.' Maybe Boon's head was muzzled by wine but he complied. As he went to enter the darkened recess he felt a hard blow to the back of the neck and slumped forward.

One of the Latinos had buffaloed him with his revolver and now gripped the butt of Boon's Frontier, wresting it from him. He pistol-whipped him across the jaw sending him sprawling to the floor.

'That's just the start, *amigo*,' Louis Philippe snarled, aiming vicious kicks to his gut, back and head. Gonzalez relieved him of his Bowie.

Boon tried to get up, to protect himself, but Louis Philippe was swinging a rifle, knocking him back. When they paused, standing over him, ready to resume the beating, the Texan wiped blood from his face and looked up. 'What kinda message you call this?' It occurred to him that he was disarmed and they could kill him if they wished. But perhaps that wasn't included in their orders?

'The message is, my friend,' Gonzalez sneered, 'you are not wanted in Mexico. You get out, you go back to where you come from. This is none of your business.'

‘If you say so.’ Boon struggled to his feet, flicking his hair from his eyes. He wanted to get in a return punch or kick, but they backed away, the older one covering him with the rifle, the younger with his own Frontier. ‘It’s too late to go tonight. I’ll head back in the morning.’

‘You had better do so,’ Gonzalez said. ‘We don’t want to kill you. But if we have to we will.’

‘OK, you win. I know where I ain’t wanted.’

Boon had left his carbine with his saddle in the livery. He pretended to be more hurt than he was, stumbling away, hanging onto the bar. But, as he reached the swing doors, Gonzalez could not resist giving him another hefty kick in the back which sent him tumbling out into the dusty street.

The two Mexicans stood in the lighted doorway. ‘Take note of what we say, *hombre*,’ Louis Philippe called. ‘If you try to go on you will never get back to the States.’

'Sure.' Boon waggled his jaw and spat blood, wondering if he had lost any teeth. 'You can count on it.' He climbed to his feet and headed unsteadily away down the street towards the livery.

What with the wine and the bloody beating he certainly didn't feel like fighting any more as he sank down into the straw of the stall beside the piebald. His head was spinning, his bones numb as he looked around him in the dim lantern light and reached for his Spencer carbine. He tucked it between his knees and lay back. Maybe he should get a couple of hours' rest and let them believe he was obeying their orders — ride back out towards the frontier.

* * *

Could he have passed out, or fallen asleep? Suddenly he heard whispering, the creak of boot leather, the jingle of a spur. He looked up, reaching for the carbine, his finger curling around the trigger. Maybe they had got drunk and decided it would be safer to finish him? Right, let 'em try.

'Hi,' he called, sitting up as he saw the two shadows on the barn wall creeping towards him. Louis Philippe and Gonzalez froze, their revolvers in their hands. But, as they frantically fired at him, Boon rolled under the stall and came up shooting. Bullets roared. The two Mexicans froze as in a frieze, their mouths retched in agony, then toppled into the hay. Boon hesitated. There was no sound but that of a barking dog. The acrid powdersmoke wafted about his nostrils as he crept forward. He thumbed the hammer of the carbine ready to fire his seventh and last shot but neither of the bodies moved. He poked them with the barrel. There was no response.

'*Señor!*' Manuel, with a lantern, poked his head around the stable door. 'Don' shoot!'

'It's OK. They're both dead.'

The livery owner joined him. 'These

men worked for Don Luiz. You must go. Get out of here as fast as you can.'

Manuel glanced around and quickly began going through their pockets, producing a handful of grubby peso notes and coins. 'You want?'

'Nope.' He stared at the swarthy, agonized faces. They were the first men he had killed. 'Waal, I ain't sorry. They sure didn't strike me as much fun to be around.'

Manuel had found a pair of pliers and was busy pulling out Louis Philippe's gold teeth. 'He was a French soldier's bastard,' he said. 'He didn't even like himself.'

'I'll have this back.' Boon retrieved his Frontier from Gonzalez's grip. He stuck it in his holster and grabbed his bedroll and bridle. 'You're right. I'd better make myself scarce.'

But there was the sound of voices and boots, men arriving. Too late! A line of five *rurales* in their sombreros and blood-red capes appeared at the barn doorway, rifles raised and aimed at the young Texan.

He raised his hands. 'It was self-defence,' he shouted. 'They tried to kill me.'

The militia moved forward to encircle him. '*Sí*, tell that to the *capitan*,' one grunted. Another hammered his rifle butt into Boon's back and they all began pummelling him as he went down.

All he remembered after that was being hauled across the plaza to a stone citadel, dragged down some steps and being thrown into a dank cell, the door slamming shut as he lost consciousness.

4

'You are a spy, aren't you? Don't deny it.' The words of his interrogator hammered into Boon's brain. 'You were sent here by your government to cause trouble. I have information that you were plotting to assassinate the state governor, possibly the president, himself.'

'You're crazy,' the Texan muttered. 'The only man I came here to assassinate killed my partner and stole our money. He goes by the handle of Ramirez.'

'Raoul Ramirez? Where is your proof for this absurd accusation?'

'Dogs who don't kill sheep don't run.'

The captain of *rurales* was nattily attired in a tailored khaki uniform, with crimson epaulettes, English-style riding britches and high, well-shone boots. His black hair gleamed, too, caked with brilliantine, scraped back from his sharp features. The thin, woven leather quirt he was wielding flashed out and cut across Boon's knee.

'The sooner you sign this confession the easier it will be for you, my young friend. Then we can shoot you.'

Boon was tied by his wrists to a chair, seated before the captain's desk. He gritted his teeth, trying not to gasp at the sharp pain. 'I wanna lawyer,' he growled. 'I wanna plead my case in court.'

'In court?' Captain Arsenio Luna's curious, yellow-skinned face split into a malicious smile as he glanced at the two burly guards. 'Listen to him. He thinks we have courts.'

The two men laughed raucously, humouring their chief, as if this was a great joke.

'We do not have courts for common criminals. Even the idealistic little Indian, our president's predecessor, Benito Juarez, did not go that far. Sure he had other pie in the sky ideas. Free schools and hospitals for the poor, shoot the priests, banish God, votes for all, emancipate women. But courts, oh no, that is going too far.'

'So what *do* you have?' Boon asked, more in a bid for time before another beating began.

Luna smiled, vainly. 'Did you not notice that line of dirty, stunted, unwashed *peons* waiting in the corridor? They are allowed to present their petitions, their accusations, their squabbles with neighbours, to me. If I should care to waste my time I will consider and decide.'

'Who wins?' Boon could not help remarking. 'The one who offers the biggest bribe?'

It earned him another slash across the arm this time and he could not help but gasp with pain. 'Agh!'

'All right, this *gringo* has tried my patience enough. Put him on the bed. We will see how he likes the *bastinado*.'

One eye half-closed, his lips swollen, his ribs and solar plexus aching from the previous beatings, Boon was not sure how much more he could take. He didn't like the sound of this and struggled as they released his arms, threw him face down on the captain's divan and secured his wrists to its iron legs.

'You won't be able to walk out of here,' one of the swarthy *rurales* growled. 'You will have to crawl on hands and knees. That's *if* you *get* out.'

Arsenio Luna reeked of sickly perfume as he knelt on one knee beside him and peered into Boon's face. 'Perhaps a handsome boy like you would prefer a more special treatment if I dismiss the guards?' he whispered, running fingers through his prisoner's tangled hair, tearing away his shirt to caress his back. 'It would be such a pity to have to flay this exquisite golden skin. I could see you becoming quite a favourite in prison.'

Boon spat in his face. 'You filthy sadist, why don't you get on and shoot me? I ain't gonna sign nuthin'.'

The captain wiped his face with an expression of disgust. 'You will pay for that, *gringo*. You will be glad to let me have my way with you. Right, get his boots off. I, personally, will flog the soles of his feet until they bleed.'

But, as the guards jerked off his boots and socks the Texan's roll of sixty dollars in bills fell out. 'Ah!' Luna exclaimed, snatching them up. 'What have we missed? Who did you rob, *gringo*? I must confiscate this evidence.'

He gave an evil smile as he slapped the thin, pliant whip against his palm. And then it slashed out burning like fire through Boon's feet —

'*Capitan*!' A khaki-clad soldier stomped into his office. 'A message from Don Luiz Vallejo. It is marked for your urgent attention.'

Luna paused, mid-strike, his arm raised. 'God damn it!' he hissed. He glanced at the guards and after he had read the note, frowning with puzzlement, he looked longingly at the half-naked prisoner beneath him, reluctant to be deprived of his depraved pleasure. But his fear of higher authority forced him to snap out, 'Release him.'

When the Texan was pulled to his feet Luna eyed him and murmured, 'Don't think you are out of trouble. You and I will meet again.'

In reply Boon drawled, 'I wouldn't relish that if I were you.'

'Give him his coat, his hat, his boots,' Luna shouted. 'Go fetch his horse. Tell the sergeant he is to be delivered to Don Luiz. Take a detachment of our men. I need not warn you of the consequences should this criminal escape.'

* * *

Madalena de la Borinella de Vallejo put her fine grey Arabian stallion into a single-footed pace, each hoof coming down alone as they sped around the corral.

'Bravo!' her father, Luiz Vallejo called as he watched from the saddle of his own mount standing outside the fence.

'Now try the Spanish walk.'

His daughter was immaculate in a white starched blouse, black riding skirt, spurred boots, her dark hair drawn back beneath a straight-brimmed black hat. She frowned as Sheikh titupped on his toes, relapsing into a fidgety false gait. 'I don't think he's ready for that yet.'

'You don't know unless you try,' Vallejo ordered, sternly.

The 19-year-old girl struggled to control the Arab and set him off again in a series of collected paces around the corral unaware of, or unbothered by the six *rurales* who had swirled into the *rancho*, a young *gringo* in their midst. They came to a stop not far from Don Luiz and watched her performance, too.

'Holy moly!' In spite of his torn, dusty, sweat and bloodstained clothes, his half-closed eye and aching ribs, Boon breathed out his admiration. 'That's some classy hoss, an' an even classier gal. Wow! How's she make him do that?'

Don Luiz heard his remark and glanced along at him, not without a certain pride. 'Practice, my friend, and it is best if you are Mexican and the art of equitation is in your blood.'

'Is that what they call this?' Boon watched the fiery Arab go skipping around the corral, a martingale making it arch its neck, its mane and tail tossing in the breeze. The rider had a look of haughty determination as she gripped the reins, eased her mount into a walk and urged it to stretch its forelegs out straight at every step.

But the Arab pranced to one side, as if he'd suddenly seen a snake in his path, shook his head and charged away. Madalena tried to control him and yelled, 'No, he won't have it. I told you.'

'Very well, that is enough for today,' her father said, and walked his horse towards the riders. 'Ah, is this the *Americano* who has been causing trouble?'

'*Sí, señor,*' one of the *rurales* replied. 'He is a bad lot. He admits he killed

Louis Philippe and Gonzalez.'

Boon fired back, 'Only because they tried to kill me.'

'This is a serious matter,' Don Luiz said. 'They were two of my best men.'

Boon suddenly met the girl's dark eyes as she soothed the Arab and watched from the other side of the fence and it was as if a sudden flame sparked in his chest. 'It was not them, it was Raoul Ramirez I was after.'

Madalena butted in, as if surprised, 'Why should you come here to kill Raoul?'

'Because he killed my partner and robbed us of more than five thousand dollars, that's why.'

'Five thousand?' Madalena gave a scoffing laugh as if she found it absurd that this scruffy young *gringo* should claim such an amount. 'How did you get that, rob a bank?'

'Madalena,' her father warned. 'Keep out of this.'

'I suppose that fleabitten specimen you're astride,' she scoffed, 'is the mount of a wealthy American?'

'You needn't insult Patch, too. He's a damned good ol' hoss. I'd back him over a hundred miles against that fancy Arab any day.'

'Oh, you would?'

'Yes, I would. Maybe we should put it to the test?'

She laughed and reined her expensive horse away, going clipping around the corral again rider and Arab in perfect harmony, showing off to the onlookers.

However, Boon was pulled unceremoniously from his piebald and thrown into a barred cell. So, was it to be out of the frying pan into the fire? But in spite of his aching, bruised body and half-closed eye as he lay on the dusty floor through the long night the girl's face returned to him, somehow giving him hope.

* * *

'Come with me, 'Don Luiz snapped at two sentries on guard outside his mansion. 'We will escort my guests back to Fronteras.'

He had entertained to dinner the town mayor and a crony. It was gone midnight and although his guests protested that it was unnecessary, Don Luiz insisted, saying, airily, that he would enjoy the night ride. In fact, he had another matter in mind.

One of the sentries, Garcia, a trusted and wily older man, had reported to him that afternoon that Raoul Ramirez had been seen carousing in a Fronteras bordello, paying with gold and silver as if there were no tomorrow. The other *vaquero* was known as Morelos, after the southern state of his origin which was renowned for killers and kidnappers. Don Luiz had saved him from the firing squad after he had violently raped a woman. So Morelos owed him loyalty.

What was Ramirez playing at? From whence was his sudden wealth? From what the young Texan had said, Don Luiz put two and two together. So, after bidding goodnight to his guests outside their town house, the *ranchero* and his two thugs went in search of Raoul.

'He's in there,' Morelos reported, after peering through the bordello's bead curtain. 'A bottle of tequila in one paw and his other groping a *puta*. I get the feeling he's about to leave.'

'*Bueno*,' Don Luiz said, stepping down from his thoroughbred and moving into the shadows. 'You know what to do. Cover your faces with your bandannas. He must not guess who we are.'

Sure enough, the tall, gaunt figure of Raoul came from the bordello doorway, a slight stagger to his pigeon-toed *vaquero*'s gait, his silver-buckled *chaparejos* swinging to the roll of his hips as he dragged a drunkenly chattering *señorita* with him. Over his shoulder he carried his packed saddle-bags as if they were precious to him.

'Hai-yee!' he cried, swinging the young whore into an alleyway, slamming her onto the hard mud and leaping on her on all fours, hoisting her skirts like some slavering mongrel. 'How you like that, you bitch?'

Don Luis did not think that Raoul would have liked the thud of the rifle barrel to the back of the head as Morelos and Garcia set about him with kicks and muffled curses until he collapsed unconscious. The *puta* screamed, but an uppercut to the chin from Garcia put her into the land of dreams, too.

Don Luis snatched up the saddle-bags. 'Good work, *muchachos*.'

He climbed back on his mount and led them racing back towards the *hacienda* where he rewarded them each with a handful of gold. 'This buys your silence,' he said. 'No word to anyone about this.'

As expected, Raoul Ramirez turned up at the *hacienda* the next day with a rueful countenance and a bandage about his pounding head, full of excuses for his late return.

Don Luiz smiled, sardonically, when he greeted him. 'Did you carry out my instructions?'

'*Sí*, your excellency.'

'You are a liar. It so happens we have a young *gringo* in custody who claims you stole that money for the mine back from him and his partner. He has come here to kill you.'

'*Señor*, I implore you, I do not know — '

'Be quiet,' Don Luiz commanded. 'There is only one way you will be forgiven: by being my champion. You will kill him.'

The *hacendado* was a handsome man of Spanish blood, with a mane of silver-flecked hair, but a cruel twist to his lips. He loved to play the puppet-master and dangle his minions beneath him for his amusement. 'Go to you quarters,' he ordered, 'and think yourself lucky.'

He had the Texan at his mercy in a cell and it thrilled him to think of the fate he had devised for him on the morrow. But now he retired to his room, poured himself a glass of sherry and took the cash found in the saddle panniers from his safe. He tipped the gold and silver pieces onto his desk arranging them in piles and lovingly counted yet again the crisp bundles of United States dollars.

'Five thousand! How stupid the *Americano* is,' he murmured. 'Little does he know I have got his mine for free. Nor is he even aware that I am the new owner. I ought to be rewarding Raoul not punishing him.'

5

'Bring him,' Don Luiz ordered the next morning, pointing to Boon.

They took him to the rear of the big, fortified *hacienda* where there was an adobe-walled bullring. 'Put him inside,' he said. A heavy wooden door slammed on the American. For moments he was alone while the *hacendado* in his riding leathers and silver-weighted sombrero, took a seat on the terrace amid the grinning *rurales*. Another door on the far side of the ring opened and Raoul Rodriguez stepped through and took a stance scowling at Boon.

'This *gringo* says that the five thousand dollars paid him was stolen by you.' The don's voice rang out. 'What do you say to that?'

'He lies,' Raoul snarled. 'I won it from him in a game of poker.'

'That's funny.' A fat, middle-aged

American had taken a seat beside Don Luiz. 'I didn't know you were a dab hand at poker.'

'He was drunk. I beat him squarely.'

'So,' Don Luiz snapped, 'where is the money now?'

'I was robbed of it last night.'

'Very conveniently.' Don Luiz's lips curled back in a smile. 'In that case you must fight. Knife or whip? The choice is yours.'

'Your excellency, I choose the whip.'

A coiled bullwhip was tossed to him and a knife came flying through the air to stick in the sand by Boon's feet.

It amused Don Luiz to act like some Roman emperor of old with power of life and death at a gladiatorial circus. He raised a finger and a trumpeter blew a piercing call for the fight to commence.

'I would back a man with a whip against a knife any day,' the *hacendado* muttered to his companion.

'I'm gonna be patriotic and bet on the kid. A hundred pesos says he wins.'

'You're on.'

The tall Mexican coiled the long plaited leather, his dark eyes gleaming as he stood prepared and grinned at Boon. 'You have no chance, *gringo*.'

'What about these?' Boon raised his manacled wrists to the *ranchero*. 'This ain' fair.'

Don Luiz gave a scoffing laugh. 'Nobody said we fight fair.'

Boon had his knife in his right grip but before he knew what was happening the leather snake came cracking and cutting through the shirt on his chest, shredding it and blood oozed.

Again and again the iron-tipped, twenty-foot whip cracked out as Boon dodged and ducked, or tried to protect himself with his manacled arms.

'Agh!' The whip had coiled around his neck, cutting like red-hot fire into his throat and he was jerked forward. 'Damn you!' he cried, catching hold of it as he was dragged off his feet and nearly lost the knife.

The guards watching cheered, thinking the end had come. But Boon scrambled up and charged at the tall *vaquero*, swinging his knife. An inch closer and he would have eviscerated him.

Raoul gripped his wrists and now it was a test of strength. Boon saw up close the white scar on the face of the Mexican, the gold-toothed gleam of his parted lips. Heavier and stronger than Boon, he was getting the better of him, twisting him backwards. But Boon took Raoul with him, kicking up to send him flying over to sprawl in the sand.

Ramirez, on his knees, pulled a hidden knife from his boot. '*Venga, gringo!*' he sneered. 'I will cut you to pieces.'

That seemed quite possible to Boon. He had never practised this form of combat. But, balancing on the balls of his feet, he held his own knife tight and outstretched. The two men, poised like battling scorpions, edged around each other waiting for the chance to strike.

Raoul did so first, the knife flashing out faster than lightning, it seemed. But Boon was ready and sprang aside, lunging back with his own weapon.

'You'll have another scar soon,' he said, gasping for breath.

Raoul retaliated with a one-two feint and struck straight as an arrow for Boon's heart. The young Texan deflected the blow with his manacles, but he was rattled and Raoul knew it, plunging his knife at him again. Boon leapt to one side, then hurled himself forward and scissored the Mexican across his legs, throwing him to the ground.

It was probably his last chance and he took it, throwing himself on Jed Joplin's killer to kneel on his knife-hand and crunch the manacles hard down across his throat. He heard something crack and Raoul's dark eyes rolled, his face agonized as Boon increased pressure and the Mexican began to lose consciousness. Suddenly something hard hit him in the face and he recoiled.

Don Luiz had hurled a revolver with great accuracy, allowing Raoul to wriggle free, half-choking, to grab up the gun. Now he could grin again as he fumbled to aim at Boon.

‘Aw, Jeez,’ Boon moaned, believing this was the end.

‘Here!’ the American roared, throwing his double action Smith & Wesson in a spinning arch. ‘Catch!’

Boon did so and rolled to one side as Raoul fired. On one knee Boon emptied the .44 at Ramirez who leapt and twisted like a scalded cat and landed flat on his back.

The onlookers were silent until the American shouted, ‘Good lad. He’s dead. Stick your knife in him, pal, to make sure.’

Boon stabbed his knife hard down into Raoul’s heart, twisted it and saw the blood flow. ‘He’s gone now, sure enough.’

He had got the right man. There was a silver buckle missing from his chap. His own heart was pounding from the excitement of the life-or-death battle. He caught sight of Madalena up at a window of the house, watching. She let the curtain drop. Boon turned to her sour-faced father. Jed had been avenged. But what, he wondered, would the Mexicans do now?

6

'He's fought and outgunned three of your toughest men so I say he's the man I need.' The brawny Nathan Blinker, in his checked shirt and leather waistcoat, green corduroys tucked into boots, was sitting in an armchair in Don Luiz's study sipping from a glass of sherry.

The *ranchero* had changed into evening wear, a traditional black velveteen suit decorated with mother-of-pearl and a crisp white shirt. 'You won the bet. Have him.'

Boon was hauled in by a *rurale*, his hands still in manacles, and stood uncomfortably in front of this incongruous pair.

'It might surprise you to know that Don Luiz bought your mine,' Blinker informed him in his Louisiana drawl. 'Raoul Ramirez had been a trusted messenger for years. He was sent to pay the money to the lawyers. But, if what you say is true, it looks like greed got the better of him. Anyhow, he's past history now.'

'What's this got to do with you?' Boon asked. 'What are *you* doing here!'

'Aw, I been here years. In Mexico I mean.' Blinker scratched at his balding head and beamed at him. 'Since '66, the end of the war. I weren't gonna swear no oath of allegiance to them damn Yankees. Came south, fought in l'il Benito's War of Reform alongside Don Luiz here. We saw them Frenchies go scuttling back to their boats and the puppet Austrian popinjay Maximilian with his butterfly net they'd made Emperor of Mexico, put up before a firing squad. I been here ever since and must admit played a small part in the regime change.'

Don Luiz, whose English was not good, had been letting Blinker do the talking. At this point he raised his glass to a portrait on the wall of the severe

Porfirio Diaz, with his thick moustache. 'Our glorious president has shown his gratitude to his old friend by the partial return of my family's lands. But my fortune is not what it was. That is why I have invested in your mine. If what you say is true and Ramirez robbed you, then that is your bad luck, but I am now the owner.'

'It's true all right.'

Don Luiz exchanged a glance with Blinker before saying, 'I may be willing to offer you an opportunity.'

Boon eyed him, apprehensively, somewhat stunned by the turn of events.

'What sort of opportunity?'

'A money-making opportunity,' Blinker put in. 'You look like the kinda guy we could use. It ain't likely to be too dangerous a mission,' he laughed. 'With any luck! Are you in or out?'

'It looks like I don't have any alternative.'

Blinker sat there like a chubby goblin and grinned gappy teeth. 'We need a fella who can keep his mouth shut, stay cool under duress and who ain't afraid to use a gun. It's a gamble but there could be a good lump of cash in it for you, more than your missing five thou'.'

'More?' Boon blinked with surprise at him. 'In that case I guess I'm in.'

'So I think we can dispense with the cuffs,' Blinker said, glancing at Don Luiz. 'Welcome aboard.' The rich *ranchero* indicated to the guard to unlock the manacles and wait outside.

'This matter is highly confidential,' he said pouring the young Texan *amontillado* in a cut crystal flute and handing it to him. 'You understand?'

'Sure.' Boon sank into a spare armchair and sipped the drink. 'I ain't likely to blab. This tastes good, but any chance of a glass of water? My throat's dry as dust.'

'Of course.' Don Luiz pulled a bell cord as Boon eased his wrists and glanced around the ornately furnished room. 'You understand, neither the president, nor the Church of Rome must hear a whisper of this little expedition of ours.'

'OK, so what's so highly secret about it?'

Blinker took up the story in English. 'I don't know if you're aware of what went on down here in Juarez's War of Reform. Priests were put up against their church walls and shot; nuns were raped; owners of *haciendas* were crucified, their lands given away to the peasants.'

Boon nodded. 'I read somethang about it.'

'There's a small town called Randillo del Fortun about three hundred miles south of here. The *Juaristas* I was riding with stripped all the gold from the church altar, looted precious artefacts worth a fortune, I can tell you. That town was practically razed to the ground. Suddenly we came under attack from the French. We retreated, abandoning the loot, losing most of our men in the process. Then, with reinforcements we counter-attacked and swept the Frenchies south. In the excitement we left all that gold and silver where we hid it. In my opinion it could still be there.'

'So, we're going to go look for it?'

'You got it.' Nathan Blinker smirked at him. 'You shoulda seen those rubies and diamonds studded in mitres and chalices. It's worth a mint.'

'Our glorious president' — Don Luiz saluted the portrait again — 'has vowed to return stolen lands and property to the church. But they are already a very rich organization. I am not enamoured of that idea.'

'Me neither.' Blinker grinned. 'So you see the need for secrecy.'

'Sounds fine, 'Boon said, as a maidservant arrived with his glass of water. 'When do we start?'

'Tomorrow.'

* * *

'To tell you the truth,' Nathan Blinker rasped out in a hoarse half-whisper, 'I wouldn't trust Don Luiz further than I could spit. Behind that old world charm he's as crooked as a wolf's leg.'

Boon Helm lay back in the hot tub, blissfully soaking his bruised body. 'So why do you work for him?'

'Aw, we git along fine in most respects. But when it comes to something big our elegant aristocrat thinks only of *numero uno*.'

'You mean like this expedition?'

Blinker was in an adjoining wooden tub in the steamy bath-house, his hairy arms and legs sprawled over the sides. He reached for his silver vesta case and struck a light for his Havana, puffing contentedly.

'I guess he has had to to survive. The crafty dog saw the War of Reform coming and offered his services to the revolutionaries fighting against the French. That enabled him to escape the grisly fate of many other *rancheros*. Then when the pendulum swung back again he backed Porfirio Diaz, clamping down on reformists with an iron fist.'

Boon flannelled hot water to his eye. The swelling had gone down and his sight was OK. The kicks, whip slashes and beating had done no real damage. He gave a sigh of relief. His ribs might ache but were not cracked. All in all, he guessed he was a lucky son-of-a-gun to feel so good.

Blinker glanced around to make sure they were not overheard. When a maid appeared hefting another jug of hot water he bellowed, 'Come over here, sweetheart, and scrub my back.' She was no problem.

'So why are you telling me this?'

'Because I need an ally. Somebody I can trust. You seem like a straight-forward sort of fella and we're both Americans. That's why I've recruited you.'

'Look, the only reason I've agreed to come along is 'cause I don't have any other choice. I've no wish to be handed back to that weirdo' — Boon stepped out of the tub and found a towel — 'what's his name, Captain Luna?'

Blinker chuckled, glancing at his companion's slim, muscled body. 'Yeah, that guy's as bent as a three-dollar bill. I bet he was reluctant to let you go.'

'Mm.' Boon made a downturned grimace. 'But I was not reluctant to be released.'

Blinker laughed and enquired, 'In the nick of time?'

'Yeah.' Boon grinned, ruefully. 'Saved from a fate worse than death.'

'Yon Arsenio does his job efficiently as a servant of terror. He's entitled to a few perks. The man cain't help his sexual tastes. You can borrow them shirt and pants. Brujo won't mind. The gal will wash and mend your filthy duds.'

Whoever Brujo was he was a fancy dresser. Boon pulled on the gaudy, flower-empatterned shirt and leather trousers, with rope-soled *huaraches*.

'To be frank I've never crossed the line before. I've abided by the law. And I've a feeling this little trip we're undertaking isn't exactly legal. It worries me.'

'Speak your mind,' Blinker encouraged. 'Don't worry, she don't understand a word of American.'

'Well, I'm just saying I don't hold no allegiance to this new president. He don't sound a very nice guy. Nor am I partic'ly religious. So, I say, OK, let's go for it. Then I want to get out with my share, get back to the States.'

'Me, too, pal.' Blinker hoisted his glistening white, fat and much-scarred body out of the tub like a whale surfacing. 'I wanna go home to good ol' Louisiana and retire in comfort. Somewhere safe. I been fightin' for twenty years and what have I got to show for it?' He pointed to his scars. 'Damn bullet holes!'

'Speaking of Captain Luna, he's still got my guns and sixty dollars he stole or *confiscated* from me.'

'It will all be returned in the morning. I'll speak to Don Luiz to send a messenger.' Nathan Blinker pulled on a clean set of woollen long johns, his cords and boots and tied a loose bow around the neck of his shirt. 'I gotta go to dinner with him so better look smart.

There's a couple of big wigs from Fronteras joining us. You can eat with the *vaqueros*. They'll be coming in off the range soon, 'cept those who are too far out. The Vallejo lands stretch for twenty miles in both directions.'

Boon found a comb and flicked his thick slab of fawn hair back behind his ears to hang over his nape. 'Sounds like the Vallejos have already got it made. Is Madalena his only child?'

'His son is in the capital. One of the president's men. As you can see he thinks the world of Madalena, so don't go getting any fancy ideas,' Blinker growled. 'See ya later.'

* * *

'So you're just the same as all the others.' The girl's voice rang through the vaulted stables startling him. 'A hired killer.'

'It wasn't like that. It was him or me.'

Boon was leaning on the door of the stallion's stall and turned to see

Madalena approaching along the tiled alley between the other horse boxes. Her slim figure was encased in a white, gold-embroidered cloak and she had a filet of precious stones across her brow clasping her black hair that flowed like a shiny waterfall to her shoulders. 'Well, look at *you*,' he said. 'Some transformation.'

'Yes.' She frowned with irritation. 'I am dressed to meet our guests. They are *so* boring.'

'You look like a princess,' he marvelled. 'I've been trying to befriend your horse.'

'Sheikh? No chance. He has already killed two grooms.' The Arab came over and she hugged his tossing neck. 'He is a one-girl horse. I have come to say goodnight to him.'

'You speak pretty good English,' he said. 'That surprises me.'

'Why should it? I have had the best tutors. I would like one day to visit your country, perhaps go to college, improve my education. But my father is against it. Women are not allowed such dreams in Mexico.'

Her arms had parted the cloak and he saw that her shapely body was sheathed by similar white, gold-embroidered material. The dress was cut low to reveal the shadowy valley between her pale pert breasts. Another necklace of diamonds was around her graceful throat.

'What are you staring at?' she asked.

'Uh — I — um — uh — you, I guess. You're some bobby-dazzler.'

'Bobby-dazzler. This is a word I have not heard.'

'I guess it's slang.'

'Who is Bobby who is dazzled?'

'Uh — well — me for one.'

She petted the stallion. 'Ah, I see, you try to flatter me, perhaps to entice me. I warn you, this stallion is very jealous.'

As if to emphasize her words the horse reared up and bared his teeth at the young Texan.

'Stop it, Sheikh. This *Americano* is nothing to me.'

'Thanks,' he replied, a tad bitterly.

'So I suppose your daddy has a man outa your own top drawer, someone with noble Spanish blood, lined up for you.'

'I am not interested in any man, noble or not. I have my own life to live. I am certainly not interested in some American drifter, one of his hired guns.'

'It ain't like that, I've told you why I came here. Anyway Don Luiz and Nathan and me are gonna be equal partners in a little expedition we're going on. It'll be a chance for me to recoup my losses. I won't be no drifter no more. I'll be able to buy my own spread.'

'Oh, ho,' she scoffed. 'Dream away.' She kissed the stallion on his nose and moved away. 'I have to go.'

Boon went with her. 'Me, too. I'm starving.'

'So, why are you dressed as a *vaquero*?'

'It's a loan.' He stepped along beside her, his heart pounding fast as he realized they were alone and there was an empty stall by the stable door. It was now or never. When they reached it he grabbed hold of her and pulled her inside, pressing her back against the wall and kissing her lips hard. At first she made no move, shocked, or surprised. Then she pulled her mouth away. 'No!' she cried with a look of disgust, fighting him off.

'What's the matter? Do you only like kissing horses?'

'I could have you flogged for that.'

He caught her by her slim waist and pulled her into him. 'I'd face a firing squad to have you.'

'Leave me be.' She pulled away. 'Get your filthy hands off me.'

'I ain't filthy. I've just bin in the tub.'

'Oh, so that's what's aroused you?'

'Waal, maybe I ain't hung like a stallion but — '

'Stop your filthy mouth.' She pointed a finger at him, her dark eyes fiery. 'How dare you? No man has ever touched me, or spoken to me like this.'

'I'm sorry, Madalena.' Boon opened

his hands wide, helplessly. 'I just cain't help it. You send me crazy.'

'*Loco*?' The slim girl pushed past him towards the stable door. 'Yes, that is the word. *El loco gringo*!'

When Boon went outside, a coach and horses was pulling up outside the *hacienda* door, a man and woman in their finery descending as Madalena hurried across to greet them.

Oh, well, Boon thought, at least I tried. Tomorrow they would be moving out at dawn into the unknown.

7

Don Luiz de la Borinella de Vallejo watched from his study window as out in the courtyard the two *gringos* and six *vaqueros* loaded their mustangs and supply mules in the early dawn. He had given his men strict instructions as to what they should do once the treasure was in their hands. If anything went wrong he would wash his hands of the whole affair. He had known Nathan Blinker for many years. He had served him well but he had outgrown his usefulness. Nor did he trust him.

The *ranchero* rubbed his hands avariciously. 'If my friend Blinker finds the church treasure, which I am sure he will, the Vallejo fortunes will be restored.'

Out in the courtyard Boon Helm swung into the saddle of his piebald as Blinker, leading the way, gave the order to move out.

'What's he grinning at?' Boon wondered as he saw Vallejo come out in his dressing-gown onto the veranda from his study.

At an adjacent open window of her bedroom Madalena, in a white nightdress, was also standing watching. The lanky young Texan touched his hand to his Stetson, smiling as he saluted her. Her face, amid its tumble of jet hair, had a serious, troubled air. She made no acknowledgment and moved back out of sight.

'Aw, gee,' Boon said to Patch. 'Looks like she's still mad at me.'

But his heart quickened with the horse's spritely step as they left the gate in the *hacienda*'s outer wall for, before them, stretched the *barrancas* and canyons of the vast plateau, the rising sun's rays flickering, setting the sky alight and turning the mountains saw-toothed pattern against the sky into purple and gold, casting the mysterious lure of the wide open spaces.

* * *

They followed a water course, just a trickle in places, dried out by the intense heat of summer, on through the rugged land. Bunches of cattle, long-horned and rangy, gathered about the muddy pools and their *charros* raced their mustangs across to shout, '*Hola*!'

Their own half-dozen *vaqueros* were typical of the breed, superb horsemen, wild and wiry, sitting easy in their light Mexican saddles, snaffle bridles restraining their fiery mounts, leather guards protecting their legs from the thorns of the high chapparal, vicious spurs on the boots that balanced them in the broad bentwood stirrups. These six, armed and swathed with bandoleers of bullets, obviously were regarded with respect, if not fear, by the common *charros*.

The youngest, El Chino — the curly-haired one, to translate from Spanish — was the most talkative and popular. The other five seemed more dark and battle scarred, regarding the two *Americanos* with suspicion. One, Sergio, squat and broad-shouldered, carried a sharp-pointed lance to fend off any aggressive bull that might decide to attack.

All were required to show absolute loyalty to Don Luiz who, not long before, had been hounded from his *hacienda* with his son and daughter. His wife, their mother, Dona Maria, had not been so lucky, dragged from her coach by a frenzied mob to suffer an unspeakable death.

But the blood-letting of the War of Reform was over. Life in this area had returned to the feudal system that had existed under the Spaniards for nearly 400 years. The *vaqueros*, their women, children and old, would be protected by their master, Don Luiz, from cradle to grave, if they obeyed.

All this was explained to Boon Helm by his companion, Nathan Blinker, who seemed in a garrulous mood as they rode along. 'President Juarez had some high ideals, but they just wouldn't work in this country,' he said. 'I mean, how could you divide up this ranch among the *peons*? You need acres of land just to support one bull. They have to be allowed to roam free.'

'Yeah, maybe.' Boon looked doubtful. 'But free hospitals and schools sounds like a good idea.'

'No, the *peons* don't trust modern doctors. They'd rather go to the *curandera*, the old witch, who chants spells and makes 'em swallow lizard tails and powdered snake heads as a cure. Schools? What good are schools to them? The *peons*' kids are needed to work in the fields from the age of ten.'

'So,' Boon called, as they trotted along, 'you think the *Indios* should be left to live in darkness, ignorance and superstition without a chance of improving their lot?'

'Sure,' Blinker shouted. 'Why not?'

Gradually they left Don Luiz's realm and headed their mounts up across a mountain range and down to join another trickle of a *rio* that led them further south. Blinker liked to start off in the early dawn to benefit from the cooler time of day. At high noon he called a halt by a water pool and they settled down in the shadow of some rocks to seek respite for a few hours from the hottest blaze of the sun.

'*Hoy, señor.*' El Chino sidled up to Blinker as he brewed coffee over a small fire. He waved a tin cup in his fist. 'I know you got a bottle of whiskey in your pack. How about you give me leetle drink?'

'If I have I won't be sharing it with nobody.' Blinker grinned gappy teeth and splashed coffee into the mug, instead. 'Coffee's good enough for you, *amigo*.'

'Pah!' The curly one took a mouthful and spat it out. 'Coffee is not what I want. We *vaqueros*, we share and share alike.'

'Yeah, well that ain't my philosophy. Too bad, pal.'

El Chino wiped the mop of black curls away from his angry eyes. 'You *gringos*, you are selfish people. You stick to yourselves, eh? You theenk yourselves better than us.'

'No,' Blinker said. 'But I know our whiskey's better than that sugar cane *aguadiente* of your'n.'

An older *vaquero*, Ricardo Gomez, who appeared to be the leader of the group, stretched out his long legs on the sand and snapped out in Spanish, 'Take a rest, Chino. We will get a drink the next village we come to.'

His face was darkly savage beneath the brim of his big sombrero. 'We will see how much these *Americanos* intend to *share* with us when we reach our destination.'

'That, *amigo*, depends on what we find. It will be up to Don Luiz to decide your share.'

'Don' call me *amigo*,' Ricardo snarled. 'You are no friend of mine.'

'Whoo! Get him.' Blinker grinned at Boon as he settled back against a rock to sup his coffee. 'Looks like this ain't gonna be the friendly li'l picnic I had in mind.'

‘Come on.’ Boon glanced at the band of *vaqueros* apprehensively. ‘These guys look kinda trigger happy. Don’t go stirring ’em up.’

‘Aw, they won’t try anything. Not just yet. They need me.’ Blinker tossed the coffee dregs away and lay back on the sand for a snooze, tipping his hat over his nose. ‘I’m the only one knows where this treasure is.’

‘Yeah, but what then?’ Boon hissed in a low voice. ‘What orders you think they’ve got? These boys outnumber us six to two. Do you think we can trust Don Luiz?’

‘You’re joking.’ Blinker gave a snort of laughter from beneath his hat. ‘That guy’s as slippery as a greased pig.’

Boon glanced uneasily along at the Mexicans. One of them, Augustin, was sharpening his machete with a stone and gave him a gold-toothed leer. The young Texan didn’t much like the sound of this at all. What sort of hornets’ nest had he fallen into now?

* * *

There was little sign of human habitation as they rode on across the bleak, boulder-strewn plateau until in the late afternoon they saw a band of riders, heavily armed, bearing down on them.

Fearing they might be bandits Blinker pulled out his Smith & Wesson self-cocker and growled, 'Get ready for a fight, boys.'

But they were a bunch of *vaqueros* from a nearby *hacienda*, who surrounded them belligerently. When they heard they were Don Luiz's men they let them cross their land.

'They might have invited us in to stay the night,' Blinker moaned, and, as the sun began its fall towards the western horizon yelled out, 'We'll have to make camp soon.'

Nor had they seen any sign of game so they had to hunker down around their fire and chew on beef jerky and day-old tortillas as darkness closed in. They had hobbled the pack mules by their forelegs so they could hop about among the rocks seeking vegetation but not go far, and the mustangs were secured nearby. Horse-stealing was a favourite pastime of *vaqueros* and there was the possibility they had been followed. So each man bedded down with his guns close at hand.

Game might be scarce but the desert floor teemed with less welcome creatures: eight-inch blue and orange centipedes with toxic mandibles; black widow spiders whose bite could cause lethal muscle cramps; collared lizards, a foot long, with bone-crushing jaws; kissing bugs in the sand, a bite from which could cause nerve damage; kangaroo rats which had a taste for a chaw of a man's boots in the night; not to mention all the other ants and creepy crawlies. But the most dangerous of all was the rattlesnake which hunted nocturnally by means of some heat-seeking mechanism in its head, was armed to the teeth with a lethal injection of venom and killed more people than any other known creature.

Whatever, it behoved any man to step cautiously in darkness and to make sure there were no scorpions lurking in the bedroll before turning in. So, after Blinker had told them he intended moving on at 4 a.m. the company settled down to sleep.

In the early hours a slight movement woke Boon and he turned to see a shadowy figure bent over his fellow American who was reclined on his saddle snoring lustily.

Anticipating that Nathan Blinker might be about to have his throat slit Boon reached under his blanket for his Colt and carefully thumbed the hammer. But he couldn't be sure what was going on.

Blinker had slung his saddle panniers onto the sand beside him and, as the moon appeared from drifting cloud, its glow showed Boon that El Chino was groping with his hand into one of them.

The burly American suddenly opened one eye and grabbed the wrist of the curly-haired *vaquero*, twisting it behind his back, rolling to his feet with remarkable alacrity for one so paunchy, and pressing the Mexican's face down into the sand, planting a boot on his back.

'After my whiskey, are ye?' he roared. 'Ye thieving li'l phildoodle.'

Ricardo Gomez was the first to wake and reached for his rifle, but Boon was up on his feet. 'Hold it!' he shouted. 'None of you move. There's no need for shooting. There's been a little misunderstanding.'

'I'll say there has,' Blinker boomed out. 'Why don't you control your men, Gomez?' He jerked El Chino onto his feet by his shirt collar and pressed his Smith & Wesson to his temple. 'I caught this dirty li'l thief red-handed going through my pack. I oughta blow his damn brains out if he's gotten any.'

Ricardo Gomez was on his feet, too, spreading a hand at his *vaqueros*, telling them not to fire. He stepped across, caught hold of El Chino, hauled him from Blinker's grasp and slapped him viciously across the face, hurling him back towards his saddle.

El Chino complained shrilly to his companions that all he wanted was a taste of the American's whiskey. He pointed at Blinker and hissed, 'You fat *gringo* pig. One day I will slit you from your gut to your gizzard.'

'Yeah?' Blinker drawled. 'You can try, sunshine.'

Suddenly the *vaqueros* burst into laughter and Blinker, too, was forced to grin. 'Come on,' he roared. 'It's light enough by the moon to ride. Let's move.'

8

The streets of Ciudad Guerrero were packed with people as Nathan, Boon and the *vaqueros* rode in. Groups of *peons* were swaying, singing, dancing, passing bottles.

'What's going on?' Ricardo Gomez called out to a man in a beribboned straw hat who was drinking from a goatskin of aguadiente. 'A saint's day?'

'No, we celebrate the opening of our church again after all these years.' The *peon* passed him the skin and Gomez took a swig. 'It was badly damaged in the war.'

'Yeah, I remember,' Blinker recalled. 'The Frenchies had snipers up in the bell tower. We blew 'em to atoms with a cannonade.'

Ricardo tossed the goatskin back to the *peon*. '*Amigos*,' he shouted, 'we are going to get *barracho de gloria* tonight.'

After the long ride across the barren plateau it had been a relief to see the greenery of trees and allotments hugging the strip of river that ran through Guerrero. And the merriment of its citizens was infectious.

They hitched their mules and mustangs to a rail outside a *cantina*, found seats at tables on its terrace looking out onto the crowded plaza and called for food and drink.

A priest in gaudy vestments came from the doors of the big church, which still had wooden scaffolding along one side, and raised his arms to speak to the people. A decade before his predecessor had been shot dead on that very spot. The new president had decreed that priests and Spaniards were no longer enemies of the people and welcomed the clergy back from Rome to resume their mission.

'Religion is like a drug to Mexicans,' Blinker drawled, as Catherine wheels and fireworks started crackling. 'They cain't do without it. Diaz is savvy enough to realize that. What's Mexico without fiestas?'

As *mariachi* bands strumming guitars strolled among the crowd Don Luiz's men devoured piles of refried *frijoles* with crisp, crunchy baked pig skins and okra in a salsa of jalapeno chillies 'hot as a dog's nose'.

Blinker dug out the bottle of bourbon he had been hiding in his saddle-bags and raised it to the *vaqueros* who were seated a short distance from him and Boon. He pulled out the stopper and took a long glug with a gasp of satisfaction.

'Wouldn't it be better to share it with them?' Boon suggested, noting their surly looks.

'Nope, I gotta show 'em who's boss. Anyhow, this would be gone in a flash if I passed it to that mob. The Reverend Elijah didn't invent Kentucky bourbon for them mongrels. They wouldn't appreciate it.'

'Uh-uh,' Boon muttered, as Chino swaggered towards them his spurs jingling. 'Here comes trouble.'

'*Haiee*, Nathan!' Chino slapped the fat man's shoulder, ingratiatingly. 'So I was right. You got whiskey.'

He held out a tumbler. 'We *amigos* now. You geev.'

'Piss off,' Blinker hissed, tapping his chest. 'This is for me and me only.'

Chino gave a leer of disgust and returned to his group who turned and scowled their way.

'If looks could kill,' Boon said. 'Are you deliberately trying to rile them?'

Blinker grinned and took another swig from the bottle. 'Maybe. They got that distilled cane juice firewater. It's good enough for them. I don't share my bourbon with nobody. Not even you. You better order yourself a beer. One of us has got to stay sober.'

When Boon's beer arrived it had a murky, milky look. 'What's this made of?'

'The maguey weed.' Blinker gave a cackle and beamed at a party of girls decked out in Sunday best, scarlet skirts and embroidered blouses, who strolled past, giggling and twirling. The American guffawed, 'Look at the way that gal walks. Everything moving in different directions!'

'Yes, indeed,' Boon replied, moodily.

'What's the matter? Doncha like the ladies?'

'I've had my moments. To tell the truth I made a fool of myself with Madalena. Made a grab for her. Tried to kiss her. We were in the stables. She weren't well pleased, to say the least.'

'You tried to roll her in the hay?' Blinker boomed out. 'Are you crazy? You don't grab a highborn *señorita* in Mexico. They have highly defined courtship rituals. You trying to make her daddy mad?'

Boon stared into his beer and made a grimace. 'I doubt she told him.'

'Yeah, me, too, bud, 'cause if she had you wouldn't be here. You'd have been staked out naked in the baking sun over an ants' nest.'

'She's more to me than just a gal. I

coulda sworn she had the same sorta feelin's for me.'

'Ah, ain't that sweet? What's on your mind, boy? I presume you ain't plannin' on eloping with her?'

Boon shrugged. 'It's crossed my mind. She said she wanted to visit the States, but Don Luiz won't let her.'

Blinker roared with laughter and smashed his fist on the table. 'You can bet your bottom dollar on that, you crazy young fool.'

Boon was silent for a bit then said, 'Ain't you ever had a hankerin' to git wed?'

'Jeesis, Boon!' Blinker jumped as if he'd been bit. 'I'd no more want to live with a woman than with a parrot. Nice plumage to admire, but there's too much screeching jabber.'

'Maybe you've met the wrong sort.'

Before he could reply to that Blinker growled, 'Hello, what's this? The cavalry's arrived.'

Riding three abreast, a column of uniformed soldiers came charging into the plaza as people scattered out of the path of their horses' hoofs. They hauled in in a swirl of dust outside the *cantina*. Leading the parade was the sharp-faced *mestizo* captain in a peaked cap and red epaulettes to his khaki jacket.

'Bless me,' Blinker said, tipping his hat over his nose and scratching at the back of his head. 'It's none other than your dear friend Arsenio. What the hell's he doing here?'

'Damn,' Boon muttered. 'This is all I need. Arsehole Arsenio.'

Blinker chuckled. 'Cool it, pal. You better not say that to his face.'

* * *

Orders were shouted and the *rurales* dismounted, tethering their mustangs alongside those of the *vaqueros* and their mules. *Peons* stepped out of their way, passers-by eyeing them askance. The president's new police force, in their big sombreros and scarlet capes, had the power of life or death over the populace and could make arrests on the slightest whim. They came swaggering onto the forecourt of the big *cantina*. Blinker had his boots stuck out, insolently, his bottle in hand, and they were forced to step over him. It was not the best of tricks.

'Do you gentlemen mind if I join you?' Mockery in his green eyes, Captain Luna gave them a smile as cold as ice and occupied the vacant chair. He fastidiously removed his leather gloves. 'Might I ask what brings you to this part of the state?'

'I'm lookin' to buy me a li'l Chihuahua doggie 'fore I go back to the good old US of A.' The bourbon had gone to Blinker's head. He was in no mood to be interrogated. 'You wouldn't know where I could find one, I s'pose? Or maybe you're more the poodle type?'

'Very amusing.' Arsenio gave Boon the briefest of glances but it struck a chill down his back. He snapped his fingers and pointed at Blinker. 'Your pass of travel, please.'

Blinker dug a parchment scroll out of his pocket and smirked. 'You'll see it's signed by Don Luiz and the Sonora state governor, no less.'

'All in order.' The captain passed the parchment back. 'Might I ask the purpose of your travel?'

'Sure, we're going up to Copper Canyon to buy cases for our cartridges.' Blinker waved a hand towards the snow-capped Sierra Madre. 'That's a mutha of a mountain we gotta climb tomorrow.'

The waiter had brought Captain Luna a small cup of black coffee. Blinker pulled the plug from the bottle with his teeth and offered it. 'Have a drop of best bourbon, *Capitan*.'

'I don't drink,' Arsenio replied, taking a cigarette from a gold case without offering them around. He tapped the end and lit it with a match, inhaling in a dandyish fashion, one shinily polished boot crossed over his knee. 'Wouldn't it be easier for Don Luiz to go over the border to Bisbee? It seems a long way to come to buy cartridges.'

'You any idea how much the price of copper has soared since they started using it for cases last year?' Blinker gave a whistle of awe. 'It's as valuable as silver these days. Don Luiz may be wealthy but he's a careful man. Much cheaper for us to get our cases from up in the hills.'

'*Un poco de seriedad, señor.*'

'I *am* being serious.'

'*Serio?*' Arsenio had the high-cheekboned, slanted-eyes look of a Mongolian. Possibly one of the Chinese who settled on the coast had mated with his Indian mother. 'I am not entirely convinced. I heard a rumour there might be another reason for your journey.'

'A rumour?' Blinker grinned. 'Aw, folks have always heard rumours, Captain. Never any truth in 'em.'

Arsenio gave his thin-lipped smile again and got up to leave, clicking his bootheels and saluting, cigarette still in fingers. 'I am not so sure about that.

Behave yourselves, gentlemen.'

'Aw, we allus do. You know that,' Blinker replied, and growled as he watched him strut away. 'Shee-it! That evil li'l prick's onto somethang.'

* * *

There were about thirty *rurales* in Captain Luna's outfit. Most such *rurales* were the scum of the prisons recruited by President Diaz to ensure that his pyramid of power stayed in place throughout Mexico. Boon Helm brooded on the torture sadistically inflicted on him by Luna and such men but any dream of a reckoning had to be abandoned for the moment.

'How I'd love to smash my fist into Luna's face,' he said. 'But I guess that ain't a good idea.'

'Yep. Curb your suicidal ambitions. We're totally outgunned.' Blinker grinned and raised the bourbon bottle to him. '*Salud*!'

With the darkness, lanterns and tar

flares had been lit and, if anything, the dancing and drinking on the crowded plaza intensified as the *peons* sought an almost religious obliteration in alcohol. Boon guessed it was a sort of release from the grinding poverty of their lives. Tomorrow they would return to their fields.

A more ugly mood was evident among the *rurales*, stumbling about the terrace and pushing inside the *cantina* to queue for the favours of the few overworked whores available. Curses and raucous laughter intermingled with shrill screams.

'Let's go in and join 'em,' Blinker said, corking his bourbon and stuffing it down the front of his pants. When he was younger he must have been a muscular man, but now his arms had gone to flab and his chest seemed to have sunk to double the size of his belly. He jerked his gunbelt a notch tighter to try to corset his rotundity. 'Sounds like they're havin' fun.'

Boon, in his more sober state, was

not so sure. He would as soon have stepped into a lion's den as mingle with these armed-to-the-teeth loudmouths. Many appeared to have graduated from distilled cane juice to guzzling mescal, the juice of the mesquite cactus guaranteed to impart instant brain damage and evil visions, or so he'd heard.

Ricardo and his *vaqueros* had claimed a corner table. They might be an arrogant, surly bunch, but they had to be given respect. Hard, proud men, indeed, but they lived more attuned to the land than the *rurales*. Fine horsemen who could handle bulls, adept with knife, whip and gun, they possessed a fatalistic bravery.

Suddenly bedlam broke loose. Tables and chairs went crashing as a fight ensued. El Chino had swung a fist at one of the *rurales* in an exchange of insults. The *rurale*, a big, swaggering brute, had smashed a bottle and slashed it at Chino's throat. Blood flowed. Chino was backing off, staring with alarm at blood on his hand. But the bottle had missed his jugular by a hair's-breadth.

The *rurale* was snarling a string of curses in Spanish, jabbing the jagged bottle, beckoning Chino to him with his spare hand. 'Come on, pipsqueak, you ready to meet Jesus?'

But it was his turn to look alarmed as Chino dragged out a brass-framed Columbus revolver from his belt and, in his inebriate state, fumbled to cock it. 'It's you who will need a harp,' he screamed.

The *rurales* were either standing, stupefied, trying to see what was going on, or scrambling to grab their rifles to aim at 'the pipsqueak' who had dared insult one of their number.

Meanwhile, the *vaqueros* were on their feet, revolvers at the ready eager to defend their comrade. Nathan Blinker, too, had his Smith & Wesson in his hand, stepping out beside Chino to grip his gunhand and force the weapon towards the floor. He stood at a crouch and aimed his shiny, nickel-plated, double action .44 at the rogue *rurale*.

'Hold it,' he shouted in Spanish. 'Everybody, put your guns down. There's been a mistake. Let's not get hot under the collar. Chino, apologize to the man.'

'To that pig?' Chino tried to drag his arm free. 'I would rather die.'

'What's going on?' Arsenio Luna had stepped from the kitchen area where he had been taking supper, wiping his mouth with a napkin. 'Do as the *gringo* says, all of you, put your guns away.' He pointed to the *vaqueros*. 'You men first, carefully.'

Blinker waved his pistol at the *rurales*. 'How about we all put our pieces away at the same time?' He grinned gappily at the threatening firing squad. 'You might kill all of *us*, but we'd wipe out half of *you* first.'

'We don't want that, do we? We are out here looking for Apaches to kill, not fellow Mexicans.' Arsenio gave his two-faced smile, unbuttoned his shiny holster and brought out a stubby-barrelled Colt. 'Do as we say!' he shrilled.

Reluctantly the men on both sides

began to lower their arms but the big, swarthy *rurale* kept his broken bottle aimed at El Chino and snarled, drunkenly, 'I'm gonna kill the little runt.'

'I am losing patience,' Captain Luna snapped. 'This argument is easily resolved.'

He raised the Colt and put a bullet through the side of the *rurale*'s head, who fell back, as blood, bone and brains fountained, hitting the floor hard.

'Nobody questions my authority.' The *mestizo* stared at his men, imperiously. 'You understand that?'

He spun round on a bootheel, aimed the Colt at Chino and fired a slug neatly between his eyes. The young *vaquero* groaned and slumped from Blinker's grasp.

As the gunshots rattled out and acrid black powdersmoke drifted, Arsenio blew down his barrel and said, 'You have no objections, I hope?'

Blinker shrugged. 'You cain't say they

didn't ask for it.'

'Right, you men, back to your horses,' Arsenio shouted. 'I have had enough of this. We will make camp down by the river. Come on, snap to it, unless — '

A sergeant began bellowing orders, jabbing his rifle butt at his more drunken men. He retrieved his comrade's cape, revolver, rifle and ammunition before following them out, but left the body of the *rurale* on the floor.

The tall, yellow-skinned captain holstered his pistol, gave them his precise smile, his green eyes lingering on Boon. 'Our glorious president welcomes Americans to our fatherland, but only if they have investment and a contribution to make. Drifters, troublemakers and thieves are not welcomed here. You have had a narrow escape. I could easily have you all dangling from those trees out on the plaza. Beware, my friends, do not push your luck for we may well meet again.'

'Whoo!' Blinker gave a whistle of relief as he watched the captain strut out to join his men. 'Whadda ya know? Strikes me he's playing a cat and mouse game with us, waitin' to see where we go. Otherwise why did he follow us here? All that about the Apaches is a load of bull.'

He holstered his Smith & Wesson and sank back onto his chair, pulling his bourbon bottle from his belt to take a swig. 'Not to worry. There's still seven of us left.'

'Let's drag them stiffies out before they stink up the place,' Ricardo suggested, and his men did so, fighting over any valuables they could find on them like a pack of dogs.

'The night is still young.' Blinker smiled amiably as a thin, bedraggled woman came out with a bucket of water to start mopping up the pools of blood. She was down on her knees and he moved his boots out of the way. 'Make a good job of it, *señora*. We don't need any more vultures than we already got in here.'

She was about thirty-five, old before

her time, worn out by work and poverty, her dark hair greying and greasy, her threadbare floral dress dirt-splashed. She worked in silence, ignoring the *vaqueros* who had clattered back in in their heavy boots and spurs to sprawl on chairs around her.

'Hey, look at the swashbucket!' Morelos hooked his boot-toe under the back of her dress to flick it up over her buttocks. 'She ain't got no pants on.'

The woman scrambled out of the way, pulling her dress down. 'Leave me, you curs,' she cried. But that only made the *vaqueros* guffaw and torment her the more as she tried to mop up the blood.

The *cantina*'s three resident *puta* had come in to see what the commotion was about. Two were extremely fat and greasy, the other a slip of a girl not much more than fourteen. All had dark *peon* looks and gave embarrassed smiles as they watched the humiliation of the swashbucket.

'What about our three ladies of the

night?' Blinker grunted. 'Don't you fancy one, Boon?'

'No, I cain't say I do,' the Texan mumbled.

'In all fairness they can only be described as plain.' Blinker puffed at his cigar. 'But they say every female has a spark of the divine.'

'It might be hard to locate it there.' Boon was uneasy about the antics of the *vaqueros*. Morelos had now hooked his legs over the swashbucket's back pretending to ride her. 'Why don't they leave her alone?'

'Yeah, I think a little old-school southern courtesy is called for here.'

He strutted across, bowed mockingly, met the woman's anguished eyes, offered a hand. 'Gentlemen, I feel I must butt in.'

A *mariachi* band had come into the *cantina*, guitars and battered trumpet kicking up a din as they went into the mournful waltz, 'Celito Lindo'.

'Madame, would you care to dance?' Blinker helped her from the floor and swept her into the waltz, one arm stuck out holding her hand in exaggerated fashion. He twisted and turned with surprising agility and the frail lady clung to him, literally swept off her feet. She gazed up at Blinker as if he were mad. And the *vaqueros*, too, watched open-mouthed. Then they began to stamp and clap as the dance livened up and Blinker and the woman performed all kind of taradiddles and fancy steps. 'Ai, yai, yai!' the *vaqueros* chorused.

As the waltz came to an end Blinker manoeovred her towards the back rooms where the *putas* had their cots. He stamped out his cigar on the floor, took silver pesos from his vest, tossed one to the musicians and the other to the *cantina*-keeper, and saluted. 'Gentlemen, I bid you adoo!'

He swept the swashbucket through the curtain and disappeared from sight amid whistles, catcalls, applause and laughter. 'Hey!' Morelos hurled the mop at the curtain. 'You forgot this!'

9

'Look at this idiot!' Ricardo shouted, as they rode out of Guerrero in the morning.

A straw-hatted *peon* was staggering home hanging onto the tail of a spavined horse still too inebriated to get on the saddle. 'Hey, *caballero! Muchas barrachos*, eh?'

The roadway was too rutted to leave any sign and Nathan Blinker called out, 'Any idea which way the *rurales* headed?'

The man rolled his eyes helplessly as the *vaqueros* cantered by, but a boy perched on the hind quarters of a donkey grinned and pointed ahead. 'That way, *señor*.'

'Huh!' Blinker grunted. 'I don't like the sound of that.'

'You figure,' Boon asked, 'that Arsenio's gonna be waiting for us?'

'I ain't so much worried about the

enemy up front' — Nathan jerked his thumb back at the five *vaqueros* — 'it's the enemy behind us I'm wary of.'

For moments a touch of panic, a lonesome homesickness, sent a shiver up Boon's spine. He remembered the woman's words: 'You are entering a place of darkness. There are evil men down there. You won't have a chance.' The odds were stacked against them. For all Blinker's confident bluster, he wondered, how would they ever get out. One thing was certain: he vowed to kill or die rather than fall into the evil Arsenio's hands again.

They were leaving the high chapparal, the desolate stretches of rock, mesquite and cactus of this vast, thirsty state of Chihuahua. The only consolation was that at 4,000 feet it was cooler and healthier than the torrid lowland and coast. Now, as they slowly climbed 2,000 feet higher, they entered a different climate zone. The agave's six-foot spires and the ocotillo's red flowers, where humming birds hovered, gradually gave way to silver birch, oak and pine forests swathing the steep mountain slopes.

'We gotta take it easy going up here,' Blinker explained as they followed a zig-zagging trail further up into the heights. 'Cain't you feel the air gittin' thinner? If you git to feelin' dizzy, Boon, don't worry. You ain't havin' a heart attack. It's just the altitude. You'll get used to it.'

'So, *Generalissimo*?' Ricardo flashed a mocking smile as he urged his mustang up alongside. 'How did you get on with the swashbucket last night?'

'That ain't a polite name for my ladyfriend.'

Ricardo laughed, gutturally. 'That skinny, ugly slut!'

'In all charity it must be admitted Delphinia lacks the sow-like dimensions you Mexicans seem to prefer. But the slimmer figure has allus appealed to me.'

'Come on!' Ricardo feigned amazement. 'You didn't?'

Nathan grinned at him benevolently. 'It's my contention plain wimmin make the best lovers. It seems they're more grateful to men for choosin' 'em, unlike some stuck-up beauties I've encountered.'

'So what happened?'

'Ah, well, after an initial awkwardness, I can assure you, Delphinia lit up like a rocket. I just had to light her fuse. Of course, the darkness *did* help. To tell the truth, my friend, she was fireworks. Thought I was under the blanket with a friggin', wrigglin' rattlesnake!'

'Maybe,' Boon put in, 'that was because she hadn't suffered a man's attentions for some time.'

Blinker wagged a finger at him. 'You got a point, boy.'

Ricardo dropped back to relate this news to his men. But the ascent was too steep, the air too searing to men's lungs, to talk much. The silence of the mountains reigned, broken by the creaking of harness, the tinkle of mule bells.

At noon they paused on the edge of a

vertiginous precipice looking out over a vast chasm. On a valley floor, 2,000 feet below, they could make out a ribbon of river winding through patches of lush crops and tiny villages each dominated by its whitewashed church.

'Wow!' Boon gasped. 'It's like the Grand Canyon, but even bigger.'

'You ain't seen nuthin' yet,' said Blinker. 'There are six great canyons like this, intertwining.'

They went on their way until the sun began its descent, blushing the magnificent cliff faces crimson. In the dusk on a steep ascent, they reached a collection of 'dobes perched on the canyon edge. The *Indios* in these parts had scratched a subsistence-living from the soil for thousands of years. Squat and deep-chested, their bodies had adapted to the heights. But the opening of the copper mine had brought them an additional income from passing travellers.

'Howdy!' Blinker swung down from his big bronco to shake the hand of an elderly Tarahumara Indian as if they were old friends, passing the reins for the man to lead his horse and the mules into a thorn brush corral. 'It ain' no use speakin' Spanish to these characters. They got a lingo of their own.'

But there wasn't much explaining to do. Nathan jabbed two fingers at his mouth. 'We're starving, pal. What's on the menu?'

Braided strings of chillies hung from the pine beam ends of the main oblong building which was made of bricks of straw and mud, plastered yearly so the rains wouldn't wash out the walls. Inside it was gloomy, one candle lighting an alcove in the wall and the statue of the *Virgen Santissima*, the Mother of God. The only other light was a glowing clay oven from which issued the appetizing scent of roast pork. '*Bueno*,' Nathan purred, rubbing his rumbling belly. He pressed a gold coin into the old man's hands. 'OK?' They were welcomed and ushered to a pine table and rough benches. 'How about a drink?'

An *olla* was plonked before them.

Blinker took a sup from the big jug and spat it out with disgust. 'Water!'

But the *vaqueros* drank deeply of the clear, ice-cold mountain water. After the excesses of the night before they could do without any more cane juice.

They shared the space with old women in shawls, muddy-faced children, dogs, chickens and the occasional lean pig that nosed in grunting to see what was going on. Other muleteers arrived, coming down from Copper Canyon, crowding in.

'Are you *Americano*,' one asked, as he ate.

'*Sí*,' Blinker beamed. '*El Coloso del Norte*. That's my home.'

To the watching *Indios* squatted around the walls on their mats they might as well have been visitors from another planet. Before the copper mine was opened this area had been barely penetrated by foreigners.

'You see any sign of the military?' Blinker asked the muleteers. 'On your way down?'

'*Sí, señor.*' One made a grimace of distaste. 'They stop at mine and go on to Divisadero.'

'Good,' the American muttered. 'Maybe we can give 'em the slip. We'll have to start before dawn. The mine is where we branch off to Randillo del Fortun. And' — he gave a guffaw — 'with any luck make our fortune.'

* * *

Boon fed his piebald a bunch of corn-stalks in the morning and borrowed a curry comb to groom him before saddling up. The sturdy horse was standing up well to the long ride.

'Let's go, Patch,' his master urged, as his party went cantering out. 'Let's get this damned expedition over with one way or another.'

At this early hour all the land beneath the trail was swallowed in mist giving the ghostly impression they were riding on an island floating in the sky.

'Where's this trail lead to?' he called.

‘Through the pass and on down two hundred miles to the coast. There’s a coupla small towns, Divisidero and El Fuerte before you git to the harbour at Los Mochis.’ Nathan lowered his voice. ‘I been thinking that might be our best way out. Get a boat back to California with the loot.’

‘Sounds like a wise move,’ Boon replied, although he knew it would mean abandoning any idea of seeing Madalena again.

As the rising sun burned the mist away they heard the thump of heavy machinery and the acrid smell of smelting copper drifted to their nostrils. Around a bend the chimneys and stamp mills of the mine hove into view.

‘When the president saw the sudden world demand for copper he took over the mine ‘in the national interest’,’ Nathan remarked. ‘Naturally, most of the profits go into his own pockets.’

‘I could certainly do with some .53s for my carbine.’

‘That’s what we’re here for, to stack

up on ammo. There's .44s and .45s, whatever we want.'

To facilitate the process the cartridges with bullets were manufactured on site so they could be shipped out from Los Mochis. At the entrance to the clanging, cavernous factory there was a store to sell to the public.

As they made their purchases of the copper-cased rimfire bullets Blinker chuckled, 'These sure are an improvement on them dangblasted waxed-paper cartridges. Every time we went into action we'd end up with faces covered in soot.'

When the *vaqueros* had sauntered out of the store he spoke to the guy behind the counter. 'You got any of that new-fangled dynamite?'

'Why, you going mining, *señor*?'

'Something like that.'

A few years before, in the early 1870s, dynamite had replaced black powder in the mines but the nitroglycerine was so hypersensitive it would detonate if a man so much as spoke harshly in its presence. The Swedish scientist Alfred Nobel housebroke it by combining it with inert substances such as chalk. Now Nobel's dynamite sticks were so docile the stiff gelatin-like substance could be sliced like bananas.

The mine assistant found him a handful. 'You'll be needing blasting caps. I'll get some.'

'Oh, yeah, what are these for?' Nathan asked, as he tucked his purchases into his saddle-bags.

The tubular copper caps contained fulminate of mercury. 'You insert them into the side of the stick,' Boon explained. 'We used them at the Shirt Tail. It takes a good knock or a spark to detonate 'em.'

'Right,' Blinker smirked. 'We're all set.'

* * *

'The Frenchies defended the main trail past the mine through the gap to the coast,' Blinker said. 'They put up a hard fight blocking our way before the *Juaristas* cleared them out. While they were busy I took another detachment this way — '

He had led the *vaqueros* along a narrower branch trail to the north, circumnavigating the great terraced bowl of the open mine where Yaqui slaves and criminals in chains toiled, and came out at the head of another more gentle valley.

'This was an alternative route to the sea and the French held this pass at that fort over there.'

Ricardo looked at its crumbling remains. 'There is not much left of it.'

'No. It was a hard battle. They outnumbered us.' Nathan pointed across the valley to what was once a small village. 'There she is. Randillo del Fortun. The French had a garrison there. First we took it. Then their cannonade and reinforcements beat us back. We attacked again, bloody cavalry charges, hand-to-hand fighting, and finally sent them running for the coast. Most of our boys went racing after them. But me and a coupla my mercenaries stayed behind at the church.'

'That wasn't because you wanted to say your prayers?'

'Nope. Li'l Benito regarded the Church as the Curse of Mexico. He had been looting them since '62. So, in accordance with his wishes, we had decided to do the same. Much to our surprise we then found a pile of coin hid by the French. Unfortunately we had no wagon to transport the loot away. So we re-hid the lot. Now, I wonder' — Blinker licked his lips in anticipation — 'will it still be there?'

Ricardo gave a shrill cry of glee. 'Let's go find out,' he yelled, whipping his mustang away, followed at breakneck speed by his men.

Nathan grinned as he watched them go. 'Damned fools don't even know where it's hid.'

'What happened to the other guys who helped you?'

'They were American volunteers in the Mex Army, like me. I heard they both got wiped out.'

'So,' Boon cried. 'What are we waiting for?'

And they went off at a fast jog leading the mules towards the ruined village on its prow of hill.

★ ★ ★

'Where 'n tarnation did we put it?' Nathan had been poking around in the piles of rubble and half-demolished walls for more than an hour and sat down on a boulder, mopping his brow. 'Let's boil up same cawfee while I take a think. This place was hit worse than I thought.'

Whatever villagers survived must have run off to start their lives some place else for the spot seemed to be eerily deserted. The church itself was roofless with only a section of its bell tower standing.

'You sure you're not just trying to put 'em on edge?' Boon asked, as he handed Blinker a tin mug of scalding black coffee. 'Just outa cussedness?'

'Would I?' Nathan rolled his watery blue eyes at the young Texan and nodded at the Mexicans who were squatted in a circle like a bunch of coyotes watching them. 'Whose side you on, Boon?' he huskily whispered. 'Mine or this pack of lousy polecats. You ready to side me?'

'Of course I am. You know that.'

'Well, this ain't gonna be no Sunday-school picnic. One false move and you let 'em have it. Remember, the only way with your enemies is the short one,' he muttered. 'Shoot 'em.'

'I'll be ready,' Boon gritted out, but his heart had begun to pound like Sioux war drums.

As if reading the Americans' minds the *vaqueros* had pulled out their pistols to clean and check their loads. By now Boon knew all of them by name. Apart from Ricardo and Morelos, there was the thin Augustin, Genaro with a black patch over one eye, and the squat, broad-shouldered Sergio, who, as well as a revolver, carried his bull lance.

Augustin was using his lodestone to sharpen the machete of Sheffield steel. He grinned, evilly, at them. 'This makes the blade poisonous,' he said. 'In the war I used it to cut one of them Spanish priests to ribbons. The Almighty would have had a hard task putting him back together at Judgement Day.'

'Hai, *Generalissimo*!' Ricardo shouted. 'Why are you sitting on your fat backside? Have we come all this way on a fool's errand?'

Boon smiled. 'Why's he call you that?'

'Believe it or not, my boy, I used to be a general. I knew our beneficent president, Diaz, when he and Don Luiz were mere captains of brigades. In Mexico you can wake up a private and be a general by noon. That's more or less what happened to me, I guess. Being from Louisiana and speaking French, President Juarez thought I would be useful in parlez-vooing with the Froggy big wigs. In fact, I rode into Mexico City by his side wearing the full regalia, medals an' all.'

He tossed away the coffee dregs and got to his feet. 'Anyway, I weren't a general for long. As soon as Diaz grabbed the presidency I was back to being a civilian.'

'I've noticed that even Captain Arsenio gives you a sort of grudging respect.'

'Yeah, the fact that I used to be a pal of His Magnificence does give me a certain cachet. He's scared for his job.'

Suddenly he spotted a little old woman, swathed in a black reboso, leading a *burro* through the ruins. There was a bundle of greenery on the donkey's back. It looked like she had been out in the fields.

'Hot jiminy!' Blinker exclaimed. 'Who's she? The town's only resident, perhaps?'

So it proved as he followed her to a ramshackle building she lived in alone. Boon couldn't follow her screeching exclamations until Nathan gave her a silver dollar and she led them, all hunched up and spindly-legged, to what once must have been a small square.

'This is where the well used to be. But it's all covered by fallen rubble now,' she screeched. 'It was never any good. Dried up, like me. That's why they've all gone. What do you want an empty well for?'

'Madame,' Blinker replied, 'that is a good question. Come on, boys. Looks like we got work to do.'

10

'There it is!' Nathan Blinker crowed, as his big Bowie knife rang out against a sheet of iron, the guard plate of a demolished cannon. 'All hands to lift it, boys.'

For the past hour they had been digging away at a mound of adobe masonry fallen onto the well but the *vaqueros* redoubled their efforts, spurred by gold fever, hurling away the heavy plate. On its surface had been scrawled in paint a skull and crossbones and the word, 'Poison!'

'That was just to put people off,' Nathan said. 'Now all that's left are these beams.'

When the pine logs were pulled aside a gaping, five-feet wide hole was revealed. There was no lowering mechanism. Villagers would simply toss down a bucket on a rope to draw water.

'It's a fifty-foot drop. We're gonna need two lariats tied together.' Blinker grinned his ancient teeth at them. 'Right, who's going down?'

'I'll go.' Genaro adjusted his black patch as a rope end was knotted under his shoulders and across his chest. 'Wish me luck, comrades.'

They heard him cursing and kicking as they lowered him, then a splashing and yells of amazement. '*Fantastico*!'

'What have you found?' Ricardo hollered down, impatiently.

For answer there was a tug on the line and they eagerly hauled up a tarpaulin sack dripping water. 'Behold!' Blinker exclaimed, pulling it open and removing a heavy statuette. '*El Virgen de Los Remedios*! She's solid silver. We're about to find the end of the rainbow, boys.'

Ricardo gave a whistle and hurled the bag back into the well. 'Fill it up, *amigo*.'

More and more church relics and bulkier items were hauled up to be placed around the well, sparkling in the sunshine. Silver plate, golden incense holders, leather sacks of gold and silver coins, statuettes, crucifixes and chalices studded with precious jewels.

Finally to arrive, clutched in one of Genaro's arms as he was hefted up to the surface, was the biggest prize of all, a sack full of gold leaf that had been peeled from some ornate altar.

'Amazing!' Boon gazed wide-eyed at the finds. 'That one village church could contain all this.'

'In my opinion,' Blinker said, 'most might have been looted from other churches in the area and hidden there by the French, along with that gold coin.'

'Who damn cares?' the squat Sergio grunted, fondling a silver statuette of a saint. 'I'm having this for a start.'

'Hang on,' Blinker shouted. 'This has got to be fairly divided. It's up to Don Luiz to say what you get.'

'Don Luiz can go stuff himself,' Morelos snarled. 'I'm taking my share and getting out.'

'*Sí*,' the squat Sergio sneered. 'I suppose you two stinking *gringos* have your eyes on the gold coin? We know you greedy pigs.'

'*Sí, muchas gracias, Generalissimo*, for leading us here!' Without warning, Ricardo hauled out his big revolver and blasted a shot at Blinker.

But the barrel-shaped Blinker rolled backwards and over and came up on his knees, Smith & Wesson in his grip and spitting leaden death. His first bullet hit Ricardo in the heart. 'Don't mention it,' he gasped out.

Boon, too, ducked for cover as he heard the hiss of Sergio's lance hurtling towards him. It cut across the side of his ribs ripping away his shirt. The Frontier was instantly out of his greased holster, the hammer tripped, the trigger squeezed . . . once . . . twice . . . and Sergio's face retched in agony as he was hurled back into the well by the bullets' force.

His machete raised, the thin-faced

Augustin leaped towards him, slashing the blade in an attempt to decapitate Boon. But he ducked and dodged as it sliced off the top of his Stetson. Blinker ended Augustin's tricks with a .44 in his back.

Guns blazed from the other side of the well as Morelos and the black-patched Genaro backed away. Mexicans were renowned for shooting wild and the two *gringos* escaped flying lead.

They returned fire, but before they could pick their shots the two remaining *vaqueros* had dodged back behind the pile of rubble and disappeared.

'Take cover,' Blinker yelled, leaping for the safety of some rocks. 'I need to reload.'

Boon lay beside him, his heart pounding, and attended to his own Frontier. 'Whoo,' he said. 'That was a close thing.'

'Yeah, nice of 'em to signal their intentions. I was ready for 'em,' his companion growled, peering through the rocks. 'They could have easily caught us by surprise later on. The sight of gold went to their heads.'

'*Greengo*,' Genaro's voice whined out. 'I am your *amigo*. I wan' no part of thees. Why don' you come out weeth your friend an' put your guns away. We will share everytheeng.'

'My *amigo*'s dead. Your bullet got him.' Blinker winked at Boon. 'You're right, Genaro. We got to stick together. A three-way split suits me.'

'*Bueno*. Show yourself, *señor*, and I will come out, too!'

'What about Morelos?'

'He's gone. I don' know where he ees.'

'Play doggo,' Blinker whispered, huskily. 'Soon as he shows himself let him have it.'

Nathan got to his feet, gun in hand, but raised to the sky and stood at a crouch. 'Now your turn, Genaro. Show yourself.' He knew what was coming and, as soon as Genaro did so the older man leapt for the cover of another rubble pile.

'You fat frog,' Genaro screamed, excitedly pumping lead after him.

Through the roiling powdersmoke Boon had a clear target, poking his Frontier through a crack in the rocks to send the Mexican ploughing into the dust. He was still writhing so the young Texan thumbed the hammer and took careful aim, finishing him with a shot to smash his head like a canteloupe melon.

They waited in silence, but it seemed true, Morelos had backed off. Where to? 'Where the hell is he?' Blinker muttered, as he crawled out of cover and peered around. 'Get down, you fool!' he screamed at Boon. 'He could be anywhere.'

For answer there was the orange bark of a rifle from the half-demolished church tower on the far side of the square and a bullet whined past Boon's head.

'Damn him!' Blinker growled, reaching for his saddle-bags as lead whined and whistled their way, ricocheting off the rocks. 'Keep him busy, Boon.'

The tubby American went jumping and hopping away in a circuitous route through the half-demolished buildings, keeping his head low, as Boon rattled out a fusillade from his carbine at their unseen opponent in the church tower.

Suddenly Blinker emerged from one side not far from the ruined church, a stick of dynamite in his fist. He hurled it at the tower. *Ka-boom!* They saw Morelos flung into the air as the dynamite exploded and the tower was torn to bits. Blinker tossed another stick at Morelos' body to make sure and for his pains was showered in blood, guts and dust.

'Well, that's settled their hash,' he grinned. 'Now we only got Arsenio an' thirty *rurales* to worry about.'

* * *

'That machete-wielding maniac sure made a fine mess of my J.B. I'd just got it worn-in to my liking.' Boon ruefully cast adrift his topless Stetson.

'You're lucky he didn't make a mess of your brains as well,' Blinker growled, as he loaded the precious artefacts into the panniers of the mules.

Boon tried on Genaro's big sombrero. 'Guess I'll have to wear this. Fair exchange is no robbery.'

The old crone had come hopping out of the rubble, eyeing them fearfully as she sidled up and began looting the corpses of the *vaqueros* of their valuables. Sprawled in the rubble Ricardo stared up at her, his eyes like dead clams.

'Seems funny.' Boon had yet to get used to the indiscriminate suddeness of death. 'He was alive an' hollerin' just a short while ago. They all were.'

'I wouldn't waste your sympathy on them gallows birds. It was them or us.'

'Didn't we oughta bury 'em?'

'What fer?' Blinker looked up at the sky where turkey vultures had already begun to circle. 'Wild critters gotta eat, ain't they?'

'You took a bit of a risk standing up like that when Genaro had his gun on you.'

'Aw, like I said before, these greasers ain't the greatest shootists. In too much of a hurry. I guess it's the Latin temperament. Excitable.'

Boon was more engrossed in running his fingers through a pile of gold coins in an embossed casket he had prised open. 'Holy Moses, we're rich! Or at least we will be if we ever get this li'l lot back to the States.'

'C'm on, Boon. Don't sound so damn doomladen.' Blinker slapped the young Texan's shoulder. 'Remember, fortune favours the brave.'

However, there was a sudden rumble of thunder as black clouds rolled up obliterating the sun and the ground began to move and shake beneath with a terrifying earth tremor which made the two men hang onto each other for support.

'What the hell was that?' Boon yelled, when it had ceased.

'Aw, it ain't nuthin'.' Blinker pushed him aside as if ashamed of showing his fear. 'It happens. The whole of Mexico's on fault lines. Volcanoes, earthquakes. Don't worry, boy. They're once-in-a-lifetime events.'

But the old woman was down on her knees hanging onto Blinker's boots, shrieking and wailing in Spanish. 'God is cursing you.'

Blinker kicked her away. 'Clear off, you old bag!'

The witchlike woman swathed in black, her white hair floating in a sudden, cold, down-draught from the mountains, was crossing herself, furiously.

Meeting her wild stare Boon shuddered. '*She* sure don't seem to think much of our chances.'

Blinker roped the casket tight to a mule's *aparejo*. 'Chris'sakes, Boon! C'mon, let's get outa here.'

As they rode away out of the valley with the loaded mules, leaving the *vaqueros*' mustangs to roam free, big drops of rain began to blister the dry earth.

'Looks like it's started,' Blinker shouted. 'The wet season. Damn! I was hoping to git out 'fore the trail gets too treacherous.'

They climbed their mounts back up towards Copper Canyon along the rim of the mining terraces and the man-made crater with its luridly coloured lake of washed-out copper minerals, the slaves far below toiling thanklessly.

'God help those poor devils,' Boon muttered. 'And us.'

* * *

Captain Arsenio Luna had fought in the War of Reform and ingratiated himself with President Juarez although he was no great fan of his reforms. When President Diaz took over, the lowly born Luna had enthusiastically applauded the return to the old order, although he had his doubts about that, too. His efforts to climb the greasy pole of promotion had not borne fruit and he was a bitterly disappointed man.

While Diaz was rewarding his cronies like Don Luiz with gifts of vast estates and exemption from the laws and taxes of Mexico that were imposed on ordinary mortals, Luna had been overlooked. He had wanted to be at the hub of power in Mexico City and had tried to pull strings to be made commandant of the capital's prisons into which any agitators such as journalists who protested about the new, undemocratic regime were quickly thrown, rarely to emerge again. Who better to become chief torturer and executioner of enemies of the state?

But Luna had been ignored. Instead, he had been cast out into the dreary northern province, to be no more than a captain of *rurales* stationed at Fronteras and answering to the beck and call of the aristocratic Don Luiz. Luna attributed his lack of success to the snobbery of the class system for he had no Spanish blood in his veins.

When he and his *rurales* rode back from Divisidero by the alternative route through the valley up to Randillo del Fortun he was in an embittered mood not helped by coming across the scene of the gunfight and the bloody bodies of the *vaqueros*. He fired a shot to scare off the squawking vultures and questioned an old woman who came hobbling out to meet them. 'The two *gringos*,' she screamed. 'They massacred these men as soon as they found what they were seeking, gold and silver and church treasure beyond dreams.'

'You hear that?' Captain Luna snapped out. 'The Yankee devils have killed Don Luiz's men and forfeited the protection he gave them. We must pursue these *renegados* and punish them.'

He looked at the illiterate brutes under his command, most convicted killers. But since the war between their countries, when Yankee lancers rode into the heart of the capital and Mexico was forced to surrender vast tracts of land to its northern neighbour, a hatred of the *gringo capitalistas* still burned in many a heart.

'Hurry,' the old hag screamed, pointing them on their way. 'They have only been gone half an hour. They have no chance. I have cursed them for you.'

Luna smiled as he led his sabre-rattling squad away. Their naïve patriotic fervour did not course in his veins. When he got his hands on this formidable-sounding treasure he would not be returning with it to Don Luiz or surrendering it to Diaz, either. He had plans for a one-way ticket on a schooner down to Peru or Chile where he would spend his days in rightful luxury. Wealth was power. It was as simple as that.

11

The rains came down with a vengeance as Boon and Blinker reached the top of the pass to join the main trail. Rods of hail hammered into their faces as great black clouds came sweeping in to darken the day.

When Nathan reached the entrance to the big smelting works he pulled his horse and the string of mules into cover. 'Jaysus!' He laughed, shaking himself like a dog. 'I feel like somebody just tipped a barrel of water over me.'

A booming and banging reverberated out of the factory behind them. The man came out of his store near the entrance to see what they wanted.

'Just sheltering from the storm,' Blinker shouted. 'Oh, brimstone and hell fire! Look who's here!'

The squadron of *rurales* led by Captain Luna had come cantering out into the main trail, wheeling around towards them. 'Get the mules back into cover,' he called, drawing his Smith & Wesson.

Boon led the mules deeper into a rock tunnel until they reached a huge hall that had been built into the hillside. Constructed of thick oak timbers, its roof and chimneys towering high, it housed giant iron battering rams to crush boulders streaked with copper, operated by the brute force of sweat-runnelling, half-naked slaves. Behind them, in a process little changed since being pioneered by the Spaniards centuries before, mules were prodded around a paved circle, called an arrastra, dragging flat boulders behind them to pulp the copper further.

Boon had seen smaller versions of such primitive machines before and here, making a colossal din, was a gigantic row of them. On a lower platform, like a scene from hell, slaves stoked fires with pine logs beneath rows of great iron vats to keep them at steam heat in order to separate, by some devilish chemical process, the copper from the slurry.

'What's going on?' a supervisor shouted. 'What are you doing in here?'

Boon shrugged and looked around to see if Blinker had followed and escaped detection. Above the racket of the machines, he heard the thunder of guns and saw Blinker backing his mustang into the smelting works shooting his Smith & Wesson at unseen pursuers.

'Is there a back way out?' Boon yelled at the workman, drawing his Colt Frontier.

'You've no right' — the supervisor gulped as he looked into the six-gun's barrel and pointed back along the aisle. 'Past the armoury. There's a loading bay. Please, *señor*, get out of here.'

Nudging Patch away, dragging the protesting mules behind him, Boon lost no time in doing so, careering the team weaving through the factory to take refuge, slipping and sliding behind the big vats.

Securing the startled horse and mules,

he pulled his Spencer free from the saddle boot and, holding it in his left hand, ran back to see what Blinker was up to. Nathan was still sitting on his mustang, backing away down the aisle, using his carbine now to keep the *rurales* at bay.

But it looked like a losing battle as the well-armed law enforcers dodged into the factory and fanned out, climbing up onto the vats and ledges to get a better pot at Blinker.

Boon aimed his revolver at a *rurale* drawing a bead on the tubby American, and sent him toppling and screaming into one of the bubbling vats. He kept on firing, winging two more, making the Mexicans dive for cover, until his pistol was empty. He thrust it back into his holster and brought the Spencer into action from the cover of a wall, sending three more soldiers spinning into eternity.

It gave Nathan Blinker the chance to whirl his mustang and scramble it back around the corner to join their caravansary, to dismount and reload.

Boon's sharp-shooting gave the Mexicans reason to pause and take more caution. The young Texan spotted Arsenio Luna directing operations from the rear, urging his men on. He gritted his teeth and took careful aim, but, as he squeezed the trigger and spent his last slug in the magazine, Luna stepped out of sight.

'Look out!' Blinker growled, back by his side and aiming his carbine at a bandoleered *rurale*, who had climbed up into the rafters to get a bead on Boon. But it was the last thing he did as Nathan's bullet sent him cartwheeling through the air to crash down onto the arrastra.

'Get going. See if there's a way out,' Blinker boomed. 'I'll try an' hold 'em.'

Boon dodged back, stuck the Spencer into the boot, and vaulted onto Patch, dragging the team of mules away, careering through halls where startled women and girls were at long tables filling copper cartridges with gunpowder and fixing them with vices to lead

slugs. Screaming, they tried to get out of the way of the angry, kicking mules.

The Texan arrived at another room with a placard over its door warning 'Danger'. He guessed that was where the gunpowder was kept. As a man hurried from the door he yelled, 'Which way out?'

Struck speechless, the armoury worker beckoned him to follow and ran off down a tunnel leading to the loading bay. 'Hang onto these mules,' Boon shouted, thumbing the hammer of the Frontier. 'Or else.'

He handed over Patch's reins and the mules' leading rope and, reloading as he went, ran back to find Blinker.

The older man had stuffed four sticks of dynamite into his coat pockets. Now, as the panicked women workers ran to escape from the fight Blinker pushed his way through them and joined his young friend.

'I'll give 'em something to remember us by.' As the women streamed out of the hall he hurled two sticks at the

rurales who had crept into it at its far end, their rifles raised threateningly.

As one of their shots whistled past his head Blinker created a double explosion which sent men's bodies hurtling into space, bringing rafters and rubble crashing down.

'Go!' he shouted. 'Now's our chance.'

He followed Boon racing back along the stone-flagged corridor, their boots echoing, as some of the slave workers took this opportunity to make a break for freedom. Blinker skidded to a halt and hurled back the last two sticks of dynamite at the armoury wall to spectacular effect. *Whoompf!*

The whole building rocked to the massive explosion, flames belching as more of the roof caved in. Knocked off his feet by the blast, Blinker was helped up by Boon and, suddenly, they were out in the belting rain.

The man entrusted with the mules had run off but Patch was leading them in a skittering dance around the yard rejoicing in the cool water from the

heavens. Boon caught Patch and scrambled back into the saddle and led the mules cantering out onto the trail. 'Which way?' he shouted.

'Back to Guerrero,' Blinker hollered, as he joined him. 'Ain' no use going to the coast now. We'd never get a boat out.'

The banshee whine of a bullet nearly took off Boon's new sombrero. He twisted around in the saddle, saw a single *rurale* at the entrance to the mine and took aim, arm extended. His bullet spat out and the soldier tumbled into a heap. Behind him flames were spritzing out of the factory roof.

'Good shooting!' Blinker shouted. 'Come on!'

They headed away, splashing through rivulets of rain, down through Copper Canyon, back the way they had come. As the trail came out beside the edge of a precipice that yawned over a giddy thousand-foot drop, the tubby American pulled another couple of sticks from his saddle-bag. He wheeled his mount and tossed them back along the trail. The mud track disappeared in a hail of earth to leave a gaping hole.

'That should hold 'em up a bit.' He grinned at Boon. 'Come on, we gotta get as far as we can before the dark.'

Back at the copper mine Arsenio Luna staggered from the entrance-way, his uniform in tatters, torn from him by the force of the blast, his face black with gunpowder, his hair hanging skew-whiff, looking more like a scare-crow than a captain of *rurales*. He stumbled over yet another of his men dead and stared at the trail back to Guerrero as he heard the rumble of yet another explosion.

'You will die,' he screamed. 'There is no way you can escape. But before you die you will suffer hideous tortures. I, myself, will inflict them upon you. You will not die quickly, believe me.'

* * *

It was a miserable journey they made, the shafts of rain plodding down unceasingly, turning the trail into a treacherous river of mud. The light was so poor they could barely see their way, expecting any moment one of their beasts of burden to slip and drag them all over the precipice. Boon's buckskin jacket and jeans were sodden, dragging at his limbs, rainwater pouring from the brim of his sombrero and, in spite of the bandanna tied tight around his throat, trickling through and down his back, chilling him to the core. The best that could be said was that by some miracle they were still alive. But how long for?

The two Americans had to stop frequently and jump down to knife away the balls of mud that built up on their mounts' hoofs, then climb back onto their slippery saddles. At one point, where a runnelling waterfall spouted out off the cliff edge, Blinker's mustang slipped and crashed onto its side and for moments, kicking and sliding, hollering its terror, headed towards the brink.

Nathan hit the ground hard, but somehow managed to be thrown clear, hanging onto the reins, hauling the animal to its feet again. 'Whoo!' He gave a whistle of relief. 'Thought I was a gonner.'

'Me, too.' Boon helped to steady him and get him back in the saddle. 'It's getting too dark to see. We're gonna have to stop and wait for the rain to cease.'

'That ain't gonna be until the end of October.' Blinker forced a reckless grin. 'Come on. The Indians' place cain't be far now. I figure it's round the next bend.'

'Yeah, and this journey's sending me round the bend.'

For the hundredth time Boon regretted ever leaving Tombstone. He decided to lead Patch and the vociferously protesting mules on foot rather than risk riding.

But, sure enough, as darkness closed completely in they glimpsed the faint flicker of firelight glowing inside the 'dobes of the Tarahumara Indians on the side of the trail.

'Howdy,' Blinker bellowed. 'Anybody at home?'

The old man and a boy came from the door and by use of Spanish and sign language Blinker asked, pointing to the smaller 'dobes, 'You got anywhere we can bed down?'

When the old man showed them to a small shack they unloaded the mules, stacking the bulging panniers inside. 'We've even got a bolt on the door,' Blinker said. 'So we ain't so likely to git our throats slit in the night.'

They put the horses and mules into the ocotillo thorn corral, tossing them some fodder, and sought the warmth of the main building with its glowing clay oven and chatter of women and children. As a starter they were offered bowlfuls of black squidgy objects.

'Yuk, what the hell's this?' Boon asked, as he tried to chew and swallow his portion without retching.

'*Cuitlacoche*,' Blinker said. 'Corn fungus.' He golloped his down, turned to the Indian and growled, '*Bueno*, eh? Much of this now the rain's started?'

'*Sí, bueno*.' The old man spoke some Spanish and raised his hands to the ceiling. 'Rain is good. The blessing of God.'

'Bit too much of a blessing,' Boon remarked, as he tried to dry his steaming clothes beside the oven.

'This is more like it,' he said, as they were served chopped pork basted with honey, and black-eye beans, with the inevitable red chilli sauce of garlic and onions, hot enough to make his scalp prickle. It was good to be warm with a full belly. At least, for a while.

The Indians, with their dark, wooden faces, huddled in blankets, squatted on their mats and watched him as he cleaned his Spencer and fed seven more slugs into the magazine up through the butt plate.

'I heard tell that Abe Lincoln tested this gun when he first OK'd it during the war and got four in the bull at two hundred yards.'

'Not bad shootin' fer a lousy blue-belly,' Blinker growled. 'An' a politician to boot.'

'Not bad! It was brilliant.'

'What are you, a Yankee sympathizer now?'

'Aw, you're just sore 'cause they whupped us. You gotta give the man his due.'

'Let's go git some shut-eye. We gotta git goin' first light.'

'You figure they'll be on our tail?'

'You're durn tootin', boy. It's gonna be a race. Them or us.'

'But there can't be many of them *rurales* left, not with the way you were tossing dynamite around. Plus the dozen or so we took out.'

'If yon Arsenio's still alive you can bet he's busy raising reinforcements. Still, we gave him more than he bargained for.' Blinker got to his feet and yawned. 'That sure was some battle.'

12

The rains had ceased for a while as they set off in the first light of dawn. Great clouds raced above them, dark and viridian, edged with silver against the sky, as they trotted their horses and mules down the zig-zagging trail. The mountains on the far side of the great canyon were veiled in mist and they could see in the distance a storm rolling in across the valley. Water was still streaming across the trail making riding treacherous.

Mid-morning, Boon heard Blinker bawling at the string of mules and looking back saw him dragging them towards the edge.

What's that crazy galoot doing now? he wondered.

The mules had their heads up, teeth bared, blaring their fear as Blinker hauled them seemingly suicidally toward the edge, then leaped his mustang into space, and the stiff-legged mules had no option but to go with him.

'Jesus!' Boon cried, crossing himself, superstitiously. The piebald was reluctant to follow. Not often was the young Texan forced to rake him with his spurs, but he had to to force him. 'Come on.' he yelled, as he launched Patch off the edge. 'Hagh! Go, boy!'

Blinker and the mules were ploughing down the almost vertical descent towards the valley bottom below and Boon was hard on their kicking heels, leaning far back in the saddle, legs braced as Patch more or less tobogganed down through the shale, swerving and leaping over large rocks. It was an exhilarating descent for Boon was already light-headed from the high altitude, and he couldn't help laughing with relief when they reached the bottom.

'What you tryin' to do?' he called. 'Kill us all?'

'We got down a damn sight quicker than we went up.' Blinker jumped down to examine his mustang that had lost two back shoes in the descent. 'We've saved three hours' travelling.'

'But what you gonna do about that?'

For answer Blinker pulled a pair of iron pincers from his warbag for one of the shoes was still hanging by a nail. 'Hold his head, will ya?'

He caught hold of the mustang's back legs, pulling it up between his knees and jerked the nail out, tossing away the bent shoe. 'Always stay hard close to a hoss when you go behind him so he can't get his kick away,' he muttered, taking a clasp knife from his pocket and cutting away the ragged edges of both hoofs. 'He'll be OK. Come on. We gotta press on fast as we can.'

* * *

Guerrero was quiet, compared to their previous visit, as they trotted their animals in through the plodding rain. Blinker found a farrier to shoe the mustang and they arranged to bed down with the animals in his barn.

'We should be OK here tonight,' Blinker opined after they had eaten at a nearby *cantina*. 'But I ain't leavin' this stuff unguarded for long.' He settled down in the straw, laying back on his saddle and pulled the corn-cob stopper from a bottle of mescal. 'If you wanna go take a look around town try not to draw attention to yourself. Don't be too long.'

Easier said than done, for the lanky, slim but broad-shouldered young Texan, with his chiselled good looks and thick mane of hair was by way of being a magnet to girls. He had left his buckskin coat and boots to dry off by the fire of the forge, but even in rope-soled *huaraches* he was tall. The eyes of *señoritas* swivelled towards him as he had a beer in a bar, then strolled amidst the evening *paseo* on the plaza. Families and children sauntered in one direction enjoying the cool after the rain, while groups of youths fooled about among the crowd going in the other direction.

One slim but well-formed young woman hip-rolled by in a swaying black skirt and a red cotton blouse half-hung off one shoulder. She stared meaningfully at him with eyes glowing black as her jet hair, engendering a stab of desire in Boon.

'She's quite a gal,' he muttered, as the woman in her twenties, who was alone, drifted away up a darker side-street.

A black shawl held across her shoulders gave her a semblance of respectability, but the way she looked back as she walked urged him to follow, unable to resist.

When she paused outside the porchway of a high colonial building to search for a key in her bag, or pretend to, giving him time to approach, he stopped beside her, heart thumping hard and whispered, huskily, 'Hi.'

She appraised him with languorous eyes, unlocking the door and stepping inside, holding it open for him. She gave him a faint smile and led the way up stone stairs to the second floor. The room she welcomed him to was barely furnished, but clean and neat. Lithe as a cougar, she stepped over to an alcove and went behind a curtain. She emerged holding a baby in her arms and fed him, without false modesty, from her breast. When he was content she placed him back in his cot.

'I am a widow,' she said and faced him.

'Yup,' Boon replied and warned, 'I'm only here one night.'

For reply, the woman stepped close and raised her lips to his as he took her in his arms. Needless to say, as they swiftly made love, Madalena, or any other misgivings, were forgotten.

It was about midnight when he came from the house and started down the lane but saw three *rurales* with rifles stomping towards him. Foolishly, he turned and ran as they shouted to him to stop. The woman had been watching from the doorway and she pulled him back inside as he reached her and hurriedly locked the door, ushering him back up to her room.

He could hear the Mexican troopers banging on the street door with their rifles. 'Jeez,' he said, 'ain't there a back way out? I don't wanna git you mixed up in this.'

The girl hesitated, then went to a closet, pulling out an ankle-length, ruched orange dress. 'Put it on, 'she ordered. 'Take off your shirt.'

'This ain't a good idea,' he muttered, but gave it a try. The dress was baggy enough to go over his gunbelt and jeans, almost to his boots.

She unknotted his blue bandanna, tied it around his forehead and, with a smile, tucked a flower into his long hair behind his ear. 'You look very sweet.'

Somebody had opened the front door and the *rurales* were running up the stairs and hammering on room doors. 'It might work, or it might not,' Boon said. 'Wish me luck.'

He stepped outside and called to a *rurale*, '*Buenos tarde*, *señor*. Are you looking for someone?'

Surprised, the *rurale* scratched at his unshaven jowls and scowled at the apparition. Stepping closer in the dim light he grinned, showing blackened teeth.

'You live here, *señorita*?'

'I sure do.' Boon's fist flashed out to his jaw, felling him, and he caught his rifle as he slumped to the floor. He used it as a shillelagh as another trooper ran towards him and cracked it across his throat.

'What's going on?' A third soldier ran towards him along the corridor, his revolver aimed. 'Halt! Or I shoot.'

Suddenly Boon recognized the tall, slant-eyed mestizo, attired now in the clothes of a dead *rurale*, a scarlet cape slung over his shoulders, a sombrero hanging on his back — Arsenio Luna!

It was only due to the poor light from a single lantern flickering shadows along the landing that Luna had not fired. He obviously believed Boon was a female.

'Hello, handsome,' the Texan cooed in a falsetto. 'We meet again.'

He hurled the rifle at his torturer, knocking him off guard, and leaped forward to grapple with his gun arm.

'You!' The thin-faced *capitan* clawed the nails of his free hand at Boon's eyes. 'What a pretty girl! What a pity I have to kill you — '

'Naughty!' Boon gripped both of Luna's wrists, but it was a test of strength as the captain's green eyes locked with his, and Luna gave a triumphant smile. Luna's finger was on the revolver trigger and he was forcing the barrel to press against the Texan's temple. Even so, Boon couldn't resist joking, 'You shouldn't treat a lady like this.'

'Goodbye, my friend.'

There was a click as the hammer was thumbed, and Boon gritted his teeth expecting to be blown to smithereens any second. Another click and —

From the look in the mestizo's eyes Boon realized that the revolver mechanism must have jammed.

'You evil bastard,' he said, bringing his knee up sharp into Luna's groin.

'Agh!' the captain cried, as the Texan got a hand under his thigh and hurled him cartwheeling backwards over the banister. Cape billowing, arms outstretched, Luna fell like a bird that cannot fly to smash onto the flags two floors below.

'He's dead,' the woman whispered, peering down at the twisted, unmoving body sprawled in the porch.

'Yeah, an' I ain't sorry,' Boon hissed, gripping her arm and thrusting her back into her room. 'If they ask say I forced you to help me.'

One of the *rurales* was coming round, groggily trying to get to his knees. Boon cracked him cross the nape with the revolver, putting him back in the land of dreams. 'So long, pal.'

People peered from their doors in the dim light as he hurried down the stairs. 'This is the *guardia*,' he shouted in Spanish. 'Get back in your rooms.'

The street outside was clear and

Boon hurried down to the plaza, keeping in the shadows, back along to the barn where his new partner was snoring loudly in the hay.

'Wake up. There's trouble. We gotta get out.'

'What?' Blinker mumbled, half in a daze from the mescal. 'What you got a dress on for? Didn't know you was a molly boy. You look kinda cute.'

'Arsenio's dead. I killed him.' He ripped off the dress and hid it in a corner of the barn. 'No time to explain. Come on. We gotta make tracks.'

Drunk as he was, Blinker had been in enough wars to react instantly to an emergency. He stumbled around harnessing the disgruntled mules and packing the panniers. 'Gor sizzle,' he moaned. 'You'll be the death of me!'

They went clipping out of Guerrero at a fast trot across the moonlit chapparal and they didn't stop until the sky lightened with the dawn.

'You say you met some woman and went back to her place?' Blinker muttered, as they brewed up a tin pot of coffee. 'Jeez! They say the quiet ones are the worst!'

'Yes, and then I killed him an' I'm glad I did.' Boon Helm stared at the embers. 'But I've had enough. I don't want any more. I never wanted to get involved in this.'

'Waal, we can divvy up now. Half each. You can go your own way. Just head due north along the Rio Santa Maria until you reach the lake, then on up to Juarez. Cross the Rio Grande and you'll be safely in El Paso and Texas.'

'What are you going to do?'

'I'll head back into Sonora. I got unfinished business with Don Luiz. There are some things a man cain't step around. But I can handle it on my own. You ain't beholden to me, kid.'

'I ain't a kid.' Boon felt tears unmanning him, his body shaking. 'I've sided you, ain't I? It's just that I never wanted to be a killer.'

'Aw, relax. You're just a bit shook up, that's all.' Nathan leaned across and gripped Boon's arm in a kindly way. 'You ain't a natural born killer like me. Never will be. Just call it quits now. I don't mind.'

Boon got to his feet, fondled Patch for a bit, deep in thought. 'OK.' He swung into the saddle. 'What you hanging around for, Nathan. Let's go.'

13

'Seems to me like you been busier than a bunny in spring.' They had been travelling all day and had hitched their animals to a rail outside a village *cantina*. 'So what other ladies you been sniffing after since you arrived in Mexico that I don't know about, you mongrel?'

'No others . . . ' An exceedingly tough goat stew churned in Boon's belly and he accepted a swig of the remains of Blinker's mescal — perhaps unwisely. For it suddenly seemed to loosen his tongue. 'There was one night.' It returned to him vividly. 'Before I crossed the border . . . in Bisbee.'

'Aw.' Blinker's eyes lit up. 'You must be talking about one of them ratholes in Brewery Gulch. The Miner's Rest?'

'No, it was a real classy joint. The

Copper Queen. That's what surprised me. This lady, she just tapped on the door, came inside and, you know, got into bed with me.'

'*This lady?*' Blinker hammered the words out. 'You wouldn't be talking about Kate Toohey?'

'She never told me her name.'

'Jake Toohey's wife. He owns the place.'

'Hell, I'm being indiscreet. I shouldn't have. If you know them, sorry,' Boon stuttered. 'Let's forget the subject.'

'Kate Toohey.' Blinker gave a whistle of awe. 'I would never have believed it. Wowee, boy! You're really intent on digging your own grave, aincha?'

'What do you mean?'

Blinker took another gulp of the mescal and handed the bottle to Boon. 'Drink up. Tell me more.'

'Naw.' The young Texan waved it away. 'I don't like that stuff. It's making me feel weird.'

'Yeah, it's like a truth drug. Peyote. Go on. There's only a drop left. I ain't gonna repeat your confidences and' — he waved a hand at the dark-faced peasants draped in ponchos, sitting like statues staring out at the rain, waiting for it to cease — 'I'm damn sure they ain't interested.'

Boon took another gulp of the evil fluid. 'It wasn't my instigation. It just happened. Well, maybe I just sorta joshed her. But she was so stiff and starchy, I never imagined.'

'What? That she'd got an inferno burning down below?'

Boon laughed involuntarily. 'I guess you could put it like that. But, no, really, she was nice. A kind of odd sense of humour, as if she was just playing with me. I never knew a lady like her could be like that.' He didn't seem to be able to stop talking. 'Wait a minute. What do you mean . . . grave?'

'Jake Toohey? Jasus, Boon, he's a real mean, bare-knuckle Irishman. Don't you know who he is?'

'No, who is he?'

'A partner of Don Luiz. Toohey's

running that mine of yourn. Well, I wouldn't like to be in your shoes if he ever hears about this. There won't be a great deal of Celtic amity.'

'God, my mother would be horrified if she knew! She's a real Bible thumper. I've always tried to follow the path. My sisters, too, two of them, I could never imagine them behaving like these other women. I always thought the only reason a decent woman would suffer that being done to her was because of holy wedlock, because she wanted children.'

Blinker bashed the table with his fist and roared with laughter. 'A decent woman? You never figured she'd enjoy it? Waal, I'm surprised at Kate. Goddamn, boy, I cain't believe it. Your naïvety.'

'What's that mean?'

'Guess. Tell me, Boon, you ain't planning on eloping with *this* one?'

'She *is* older than me,' Boon mused. 'But we kinda clicked. Whereas Madalena, well, I love her, too, but she's awful kinda haughty.'

'Haughty? What do you expect her to be?' Boon bellowed. 'She's been waited on hand and foot all her life. She don't even comb her own hair. She has a maid to dress her. You know somethang, pal? I can't see either of them dames takin' to being a sodbuster's wife in the wilds of Coloradey.'

The last Boon Helm remembered, before the effects of the mescal knocked him backwards off his stool, was the sight of Blinker's back teeth as he went into more maniacal laughter . . .

* * *

Boon had bought a white cotton shirt and a densely-woven striped poncho to keep off the worst of the rain from an Opata squaw who squatted outside the *cantina* with her items for sale.

As they left, her man lurched off before them, called to her, slung a leg over his *burro* and ambled away. The woman tied up her huge bundle, hoisted it onto her head, and waddled away through the mud after him.

'That's typical Mexico,' Blinker said, pulling on his ex-Confederate Army greatcoat with its water-proofed cape. 'The beast carries the man and the woman the burden. They sure got their priorities right. None of that women's rights nonsense down in these parts.'

It was just a village of mud hovels, with muddy inhabitants, but they would be able to rent rooms in the *jacals* to rest awhile.

⋆ ⋆ ⋆

When they set out, the Rio Burispe had been almost dry. Now it had become a turbulent, bubbling force filled with debris as the summer monsoon caused great landslides washing boulders down from the high Sierra Madre to swell its waters.

They had left Chihuahua, entering the state of Sonora and the realm of *el grande ranchero*, Don Luiz, was not far away.

'Did you know that seventeen grandees own ninety-six million acres, a fifth of the total area of Mexico?' Blinker waved a hand at the countryside. 'Diaz has rewarded his toadies. So much for the wonderful revolution.'

'Why so embittered, Nathan? Didn't you get a share?'

'I got paid for being a mercenary. Sure, I had a good time while Juarez was alive. He treated me fairly. I helped Don Luiz establish himself and he was not ungenerous. But what did I get for doing his dirty work compared to him? Peanuts! President Diaz is never going to grant much in the way of favours to non-Mexicans.'

'So, you believe we are entitled to our little bonus?'

'Certainly, and more. Don Luiz will have to pay through the nose what he owes me before I head for the border.'

Boon did not like the sound of this. But what could he do? He could not back out now. He was not a religious man. The Church had reigned supreme here for hundreds of years while millions of the Indios were slaughtered before it had even been allowed, quite recently, that such people might conceivably possess souls. Nonetheless, he was not happy with the theft of these church treasures. It made him feel somehow dirty.

As the rain hammered down again, and they followed the river north, he felt as if he was heading into a maelstrom that could only end in more bloodshed and, in all probability, their own deaths.

* * *

They had a hard time crossing the river, nearly losing one of the mules with its precious cargo to the raging torrent. On the far side they paused for breath, emptying the water from their boots as the sun came out from the clouds again.

'Hey, look at this.' Boon peered at a teeming scorpions' nest. In its centre two of the creatures, a menacing three inches long, were darting about each other, tails raised. 'The dance of the scorpions,' he marvelled. 'I've heard it can lead to sex or death. Or both.'

'Yeah? That's probably what you're headed into, boy,' Blinker growled grimly, swinging back onto his saddle.

Not long after, a bunch of riders appeared on the horizon and, as they got closer, Boon's heart missed a beat when he realized that one of them was Madalena Vallejo, galloping her grey stallion across the rocky terrain to meet them. He could only admire the way she seemed to be moulded to the horse's movement, hanging low over the Arab's neck, her hair in a long ponytail streaming back like the stallion's mane and tail, leading the thundering bunch of *vaqueros*, bringing Sheikh to a halt with fingertip control.

'We meet again, *señorita*,' Boon cried, smiling to see the surprise on Madalena's face.

'You!' The girl appeared shocked. 'I

did not recognize you in your sombrero. I did not expect to see you again.'

'Why not? I've come back to take you away. How'd you like to ride north of the border with me?'

'With you?' She stared at him over the head of the powerful beast between her legs. 'Are you mad?'

Blinker was more bothered by an older *vaquero*, Alberto, one of Don Luiz's trusted henchmen, who was riding around the mules eyeing their cargo. 'Keep your nose outa that,' he shouted. 'It is for the eyes of Don Luiz only.'

Alberto returned his stare, his face snapping hard shut like a rat-trap. He fingered the trigger of the rifle across his knee but wheeled his mustang away.

Blinker muttered, 'I seen the same look in the eyes of a rattlesnake I trod on once.'

'We took you for *bandidos*.' Today Madalena was attired in a blouse and split leather riding skirt, her hard-brimmed hat dangling on her back.

'Why is it you look more like some dirty, drifting saddle-tramp than you did before?'

Boon laughed and scratched at the blond beard around his jaws. 'And how come you look more beautiful than I last remember you?'

Madalena gave a scornful, flashing smile and turned the stallion to ride alongside him. 'So the impudent *gringo* still thinks he can try his luck with me? You're joking, of course.'

'Nope. I told ya I was going to start a ranch up in Colorado. Now I got the wherewithal. So, I'm asking why doncha come with me. Marry me.'

'You *are* mad.' There was an arrogance to the proud tilt of her head as she shied away. 'Do you really think my father would allow that?'

'Don't see how he can stop you.'

'Don't you?' she said. 'Then you are more of a fool than I took you for.'

'Grow up, Boon,' Blinker butted in, as they headed into the high gateway of the *hacienda* manned by its armed guards. 'I think Don Luiz's got other plans for us.'

And there he was, on the veranda of his study, looking down at them as they clattered into the paved courtyard, giving a regal wave. 'So, you made it,' he called. 'Arturo, bring those panniers up to my study, untampered with, you understand?'

'*Sí, señor*,' Arturo sang back, and sprang down to start unloading the mules.

'Your father sure likes giving the orders,' Blinker complained to the girl.

'Why shouldn't he?' Madalena replied. 'He is in charge.'

'I wouldn't be so sure about that,' Blinker growled, patting the butt of the self-cocker on his belt.

Stiff and saddle-sore, he grabbed a tarpaulin pannier and led the way into the house and up to Don Luiz's palatial study. He slung it onto the landowner's wide desk. 'You'll see I've kept my word.'

Don Luiz could hardly wait to dismiss Arturo, snapping, 'Wait outside.'

As soon as the door was locked he delved into the bag on his desk, giving a sigh of awe as he pulled out a ruby-studded chalice and, from the bottom of the bag, the thin sheets of pure gold. 'You were right,' he cried.

'I sure was,' Blinker gruffly replied. 'So, I'm prepared to be generous. I'll split this half an' half with you, then me an' Boon will be on our way.'

Don Luiz stroked a hand through his silver hair and laughed, almost incredulously. 'So, where are Ricardo and the others?'

'They tried to murder us. But they didn't have no luck.' Blinker eyed the *hacendado* with an angry glint in his eye, and bluffed, 'Before he died Ricardo told me he was acting on your orders.'

'My dear old friend,' Don Luiz protested. 'That is absurd. You and I, we go back a long way.'

'Yeah, that's what's got me riled. Anyhow, it weren't a good idea. They're all dead. In fact a lot of men died trying to stop us getting this stuff back here.'

'Father, what is going on?' Madalena suddenly demanded. 'What are all these valuable church relics? Why all this talk of killing?'

'The spoils of war, my dear. Worth a fortune to our family, I would say. There is nothing for you to worry about.'

'Why doncha tell her the truth? That you're a double-crossing snake. Allus have been. But you ain't gonna crawfish me this time, Don Luiz.' Nathan Blinker had his Smith & Wesson out and pointed at the *ranchero*. 'Before we terminate our partnership I'm gonna look in your safe. You'd better step over there outa the way, girl.'

Blinker pushed her to one side as he went around the desk and jammed his revolver into Don Luiz's throat. He frisked him and pulled a key from the pocket of his suit. 'Boon,' he called. 'Keep an eye on him. He's as slippery as an eel.'

He unlocked a big iron safe, rifled

through the contents and growled, 'Ah, this looks like the moolah.'

He placed a wad of US treasury notes on the desk. 'Boon, where's that bit of paper you showed me with all the numbers of the stolen notes written down?'

The Texan fumbled in his coat pocket and passed a dirty bit of paper across. 'My partner, Jed Joplin, was a careful man.'

Blinker flicked through the greenbacks. 'All these numbers match.'

'They *do*? This money was a debt repaid me,' Don Luiz protested. 'I had no idea.'

'And these?' Blinker hoisted two leather bags of clinking coins out of the safe and onto the table. 'Full of United States coin. Look familiar, Boon?'

'Yes,' Boon said. 'The pouches Jed kept our savings in. Stolen by his murderer.'

Don Luiz had sunk back into the chair of his desk. 'I swear I had no knowledge of that.'

'This cash belongs to Boon and he's taking it back.' Blinker waggled his revolver under Don Luiz's aristocratic nose. 'I'll be taking the bags of coin we found in the well and the sheets of gold. You can keep the bulky stuff, Don Luiz. I figure it's more than you deserve, you lousy double-crossing sonuvabitch.'

'You're a fat fool, Nathan. Just how do you think you're going to walk out of here?'

'*She's* coming with us.' Blinker pulled a piece of cord from his pocket and tossed it to Boon. 'Tie her wrists before her. Go on, man. *Move!* You're in this all the way.'

Madalena fought back, shrilly protesting, until Blinker intervened and slapped her viciously, back and forth across her face. 'Shut up, you stuck-up bitch. You've had it too easy all your life. Now's payback time.'

'Hey!' Boon grabbed his arm. 'That's enough!'

Blinker shook him off, grabbed the girl by her pony-tail, doubled her up and stuck the Smith & Wesson barrel in her mouth. 'Suck on that. You scream or make one false move an' you're dead.'

'Come *on*,' Boon shouted. 'There's no need for this.'

Blinker glowered at him. 'Whose side you on? Are you with me or not? I ain't got no qualms about killin' a woman. Not if she stands 'tween me and my cash. She wouldn't be the first.'

The startled young Texan had never seen this side of Blinker. Madalena was gagging on the gun. It was a hair-trigger situation. 'I'm with you,' he said. 'Just calm down.'

'Then get her tied.' Blinker hurled the girl at him. 'I'm giving the orders now.'

Suddenly Boon realized that Don Luiz was sneaking open his desk drawer, coming out with a silver-engraved revolver aimed at Blinker. As the don's shot cracked out, true to his Texan instincts Boon's Frontier was in his grasp, the hammer thumbed, his bullet smashing into the *rancheros* forearm.

Blinker yelped and spun around as Don Luiz grimaced with pain, dropping the revolver. 'I oughta kill you.' He kicked the revolver away into a corner. 'You wanna see your daughter alive again you'd better start telling your boys what they gotta do. One false move an' she's dead.'

The *vaqueros* on guard outside were already hammering on the locked study door. '*Señor*,' one called. 'Are you all right?'

Blinker glanced at a crease of blood across his belly leaking from the shirt. 'Lucky for you it's only a scratch,' he growled at Don Luiz, as he laid the Smith & Wesson aside on the desk top while he sorted Boon's notes and coin into one pannier and placed the gold sheet and sacks of coin from the well into the other.

'Keep hold of that wildcat,' he called over his shoulder to the Texan. 'First man through that door, kill him.'

Blinker took out his knife and started prising sapphires and rubies from the silver chalice, tipping them into his pocket. 'Might as well have a few of these. We'll only need one mule now.

'You'll never get away with this,' Madalena cried.

'Honey, for your sake we better had. Here's the plan.' Nathan took a rope from a pannier and noosed it around her slim neck, tossing the end to Boon. 'Hang onto that. She can ride her Arab. It's thirty miles to the border. Once we're safely over the line she'll be released and free to return. That's the set-up. Got it?'

Don Luiz nodded, abjectly, holding his shattered arm. 'I will instruct my men.'

Blinker grinned at them. 'It's amazing what fat fools an' drunks can git away with. You know why? 'Cause they're the only ones crazy enough to try!'

Suddenly the door lock was cracking away and Arturo burst in, his revolver flashing fire at Nathan, who crouched, ready for him, his return shot stoving in the Mexican's forehead.

A big *vaquero* charged, rifle reverberating. This time Boon gave no mercy. He tripped the hammer of the Frontier and a cartridge ball pounded into the man's cheek, snapping back his head. He tumbled dead on top of Arturo and Boon recognized him as Brujo, the man who had loaned him his shirt.

As blue gunsmoke roiled and churned he thumbed the hammer again. It was not just a matter of protecting himself but the girl. He held her back against the wall, but a third *vaquero*, the older man, Garcia, was more discreet, calling from the doorway, 'What's going on, *señor?*'

'Put away your guns,' Don Luiz gasped out. 'The *gringos* are leaving. They are taking Madalena. Nobody is to interfere. You understand?'

'He better,' Nathan muttered. 'Hey, Garcia, carry these two panniers down to the courtyard. Load up one mule. Tell everyone to throw down their weapons. Come on, let's go.'

'Tell everybody,' Don Luiz gritted out. 'The *gringos* are riding out of here with Madalena. Do not attempt to stop them. If a hair of her head is harmed whoever is responsible will never live to tell the tale.'

'Move.' Blinker gave the girl a push. 'Let's hope for your sake they follow your father's advice.'

They descended the stairs, holding the noosed girl tight, revolvers ready, but *vaqueros* stood back and let them pass. Out into the courtyard, swinging onto their horses, watching the girl mount her Arab, led by Boon, Blinker holding onto the mule's rein, they cantered out to the main gate.

But the sombrero'd sentry on the watch tower had misunderstood the situation. He raised his rifle and fired at Boon. As the bullet spat past his ear the Texan spun around in the saddle and took out the sentry with his fist shot. He tumbled from the tower to hit the ground hard.

'Yagh!' Blinker put spurs to his mustang and led them at a gallop across the high chapparal towards the north, yelling farewell to Mexico. '*Vamos, muchachos*!'

14

'That was a tight necktie,' Nathan Blinker admitted as they passed the rock that marked 'the line' and gradually reined in. 'But we're back in the good ol' US of A.'

Boon glanced behind and saw that Garcia and his band of *vaqueros* who had followed them had halted, too, a quarter of a mile away. He jumped down from Patch and took a mouthful of water from his canteen, offering it to Madalena who had joined him on the ground.

'You're free.' He gently removed the noose from her neck and cut her wrist bonds. 'You coming with me? Or going back?'

The Mexican girl tossed her head, angrily. 'What do you think?' She stepped closer and briefly kissed his lips, but as she did so the spirited Sheikh reared up, flailing his forehoofs at the Texan, who dodged back. 'Hell!'

'That's your answer.' Madalena spoke sternly to the jealous stallion and swung lithely aboard. '*Adios*,' she called, as she sent him sprinting back towards her followers.

'That hoss thought three might be a crowd,' Blinker cackled as they watched her go. 'Her daddy might not have approved of you either, as a son-in-law.'

Boon frowned and patted the piebald's neck. 'Come on, old pal, you done well. It ain't far to Douglas now. We'll get some rest.'

'Yes, siree,' Nathan whooped. 'I cain't wait to chaw on a slice of real American blueberry pie. It's good to be home and dry.'

* * *

At noon the next day they rode into Bisbee, past the thumping machinery of the copper mines, through the town until they reached The Copper Queen.

'I'd advise you to ride on by,' Blinker grunted out. But Boon had seen Kate Toohey come out onto the hotel veranda and stare at them in astonishment. He could not resist gigging the piebald up close.

'If it ain't the wandering cowboy.' She looked as neat and prim as ever in her ankle-length skirt and blouse buttoned tight across her bosom. Her face lit up with a smile, although he noticed a blue bruise on her cheek. 'So you're still alive?'

Boon grinned at her. 'Just.'

'Can I serve you gentlemen a jug of beer?'

He knew he should refuse but the mischievous gleam lurking in her blue eyes, the curves of her body's stance juddered a jerk of desire through him. 'Why not?'

He vaulted from the saddle onto the veranda. 'Like you warned me,' he said, unable to unlock his eyes from hers, 'I've been to hell and back. But I've got what I went for, the cash they stole from Jed. I guess it's mine now he's dead. And he's avenged. That's good enough for me.'

'I'm glad,' she whispered, huskily. 'Glad you're alive. I've been worried.'

'What's that?' he asked, touching her cheek. 'You been in the wars, too?'

'I'm a married lady; it ain't a lot of laughs.' Kate Toohey made a grimace of distaste. 'He knocks me around. But he'd never let me go. Oh, my God! Here he is. You better clear out quick. Somebody told him about us.'

Patrick Toohey had come riding up out of the canyon from the direction of Tombstone. Unfortunate timing, but perhaps it was foreordained, it occurred to Boon.

He was a powerful-built man, chest and shoulders bulging under a neat suit, 'the map of Ireland written all over him', as they say, curly-haired and florid of face. He rode up to the hotel and glowered at them as he stepped down from the mare, tossing the reins to a groom. 'Did I see ye with your hand touching my wife?' he demanded aggressively.

The Texan faced him, sensing the menace in the man. 'I'm just passing through. I'll bid you good day.'

'Yes, I've an idea you passed through here, or should I say *her*, before.' The Irishman climbed steps to the hotel's main entrance but took a stance about thirty paces away. He unbuttoned his suit jacket to reveal a heavy Paterson revolver holstered across his loins. 'Would your name be Boon Helm, boy? If so, you can kiss goodbye to all you got.'

'That's me.' Boon licked his lips, nervously, pushing the woman to one side out of harm's way. 'There's no need for this.'

'No man touches my wife,' Toohey roared, in his thick Irish tones. He dragged out the .45 and it was kicking in his hand with each wild shot. Boon had brought up his Frontier but one of the whining slugs knocked it spinning from his grasp. As the gunsmoke cleared he realized that Toohey might be out of lead and, surprisingly, *he* was unscathed. But for how long?

'No!' Kate screamed. 'Pat, don't! He's unarmed.'

'To be sure.' Toohey tossed the Paterson five-shot towards him and it clattered along the boards. 'Maybe there's a bullet left in it. Maybe not. Pick it up, you yellow cur. Let's find out.'

He pulled a Remington .36 from a shoulder holster beneath his jacket. 'I'm gonna enjoy shooting the holy hell out of you.'

Blinker was still sitting his mustang, watching and waiting. 'Yeah, you do that, Patrick,' he growled. 'But first, what about me?'

'Goddamn! You!' Toohey turned and fired, but as bullets blasted out from both men's guns there was barely time for a prayer. The Irishman backpedalled and was bowled over to sprawl in the hotel doorway.

Kate ran to kneel beside him,

touching the bloody hole in his forehead. 'Oh, Jesus,' she cried. 'He's dead.'

Boon Helm was watching Blinker as he slowly tumbled from the saddle and hit the mud. He jumped down to him. Blood was pumping from his chest. Blinker stared at him with watery eyes. 'I couldn't let him kill ya, could I, pard?'

'Get a doctor,' Boon called, trying to plug the wound with his bandanna as the Mexican groom ran up and diners came to gawp from the door of the hotel.

'Sawbones won't be no good to me,' Blinker gasped out. 'I'm going.' He stared up at the blue sky as his blood trickled through Boon's fingers. 'I'd like to have come to Coloradee with you . . . snowy mountains . . . pine trees . . . peace an' — ' His eyes glazed over.

Boon closed them with his fingers, muttering, 'Sure . . . '

⋆ ⋆ ⋆

'I was eating in the restaurant an' saw the whole thing through the window,' the Bisbee sheriff told him. 'Pat Toohey always was a hothead. You're free to go, but I'd advise you not to come back. He had a lot of friends.'

'I'll leave the mule and his stuff in the panniers. I don't want nothing to do with it.'

The bodies had been covered up and the scene had quietened, the rubber-neckers drifting away.

'I'm sorry,' Boon said to her. 'What will you do?'

Kate Toohey gave a wistful smile and shrugged. 'I guess I'll be a wealthy widow now. If you're ever back this way . . . '

'No, I don't think that's likely.'

'Well, in a month or so, if you're settled you could write to me. Who knows, maybe — '

'Maybe.' The young Texan pressed her hand, then went to jump on his piebald, which reared on his backlegs, eager to be away. 'So long,' he called and headed down into the canyon and on up the trail. It was good to be free, to be alive. A new world stretching before him.

THE END